Shadow's Moon

Season Two

Chasing a dream

Shadow's Moon

Ash Rock Series
Marcelle Valentine

 Medusa Publishing

Table of Contents

Episode Twenty-Nine: Slang

Shay

ALL THINGS CONSIDERED, I have to say my first party sucked, and my first one has decidedly been my last.

After sneaking away, I shifted and ran like the devil was chasing me since I fully realized I was on their pack land. I admit it surprised me I was able to traverse across their lands without being harassed by their scouts or sentries. Had these lands belonged to either Tobias or his brother Sebastian, they would have had the entire pack out hunting me down.

Ness showed up at my house the next day, but I didn't feel like explaining myself or why I left, so I elected not to answer the door. Since I don't have a phone, she can't call me, and tonight is the first night I've had another shift which kept her from confronting me at work.

Hopefully, a typical Monday night at Stooges doesn't include hosting any other tournaments, card games, or surprise birthday parties. And I'm really praying Foster doesn't come in. Fingers crossed, the Moon Goddess is in a giving mood today and grants me this one little wish.

I know I'll have to see all of them tomorrow during the tournament, which is fine since there is no way I am letting anyone talk me into competing. My ass is staying behind the bar where it belongs this time.

The only outstanding issue I have lingering from the party is I was in such a hurry to get out of his house I forgot my coat. The weather has been unseasonably warm, so it shouldn't be an issue. At least, I hope it isn't an issue. Goddess, please don't let this be an issue. There is no way I have the funds right now to replace anything.

Walking into work, I am immediately greeted by Hyde. I am not left wondering long where my favorite boss is when I hear something fall in the kitchen, followed by his booming voice yelling something in his Irish slang. Yep, totally not even going to try to figure out what he just said.

"Hey, kiddo, how was the party? Did you end up sleeping off a hangover all day yesterday?" I don't really have the heart to tell him what a terrible time I had, especially since I practically gushed about it all day on Saturday. Not really knowing how to answer this without making myself look like a whiny asshole, I do the best thing I can think of; I smile and give him a slight shrug of my shoulders.

Jerry's here and is well on his way to being shit-faced. Since I started here, I have discovered Seamus makes sure Jerry gets home safely every night. I guess Jerry hasn't always been like this; he didn't start drinking until his wife passed away suddenly, and he couldn't stand being alone in their house. He's a sweet guy who doesn't seem to have a mean bone in his body. I wonder if this is a requirement to be considered a regular here at Stooges since I could say the same thing about Hyde.

An hour after I arrived at work, Mandy came breezing in looking like a million bucks.

"Hi, Shay. Are you ready for a fun-filled night?"

"Sure, as long as you tell me, the fun-filled part doesn't include crazy tournaments that bring half the town with it."

"If it does, will it send you running? Because if you're planning on running, then my answer is nope, nothing crazy." She grins before winking while my eyes go wide at her revelation. Shit, does this mean something is going on here tonight? Oh, man, I don't know if I'm ready for another night like Tuesday. Hyde felt bad and clued me in on Mandy's teasing.

Before the bar got too busy, I filled the stock and helped Seamus in the kitchen. Mandy yelled an order for four burgers and fries into us. I decided to help Seamus fill this order before checking to see if Mandy needed any help.

Seamus teased me, or as he says, slag me the entire time I was in the kitchen. He had me in stitches as he tried to teach me some of his Irish slang. It seems if I have to use the bathroom here in the States, then over in Ireland, I have to use the bog. Snogging is kissing and take the piss over there absolutely does not mean the same thing it does here since this is another way to say he's teasing me.

I also asked what Tichy meant since this is what he kept calling me the entire time he was showing me the house. Apparently, his mom gave him this nickname as a kid and continued calling him it throughout his teens. From what

Seamus explains, she said it in jest; the joke being this word means tiny. I can promise you this Seamus is anything but tiny.

Grabbing the plates of food, I grin as I tell him I'll see him later, and of course, I can't help calling him Tichy. Which garners a booming laugh from the big guy.

Juggling the plates filled with the wonderfully delicious burgers, I am hit by the smell long before I see them, and my heart sinks. Foster is here. Worse than him just being here, I realize these damn burgers I am taking out belong to his table. I admit I need a second to calm my racing heart and get my breathing back under control.

Here's hoping Ness isn't here because as long as she is not here, I can probably just set the plates down and skedaddle my ass right back behind the bar without saying a word. But as I round the bar, I know none of my prayers have been answered since not only is Ness here but so are Finch and Lindsey.

"Shay," I see Foster's back stiffen upon Ness calling out my name. Damn, I get it. You don't want anything to do with me; well, let me assure you, mister, the feeling is mutual. "why the hell did you leave? I told you I would take you home."

"It was a pleasant night. I didn't mind the walk. Besides, I would have felt like a bum making you leave after we just got there."

"It's like a two-hour walk, Shay." Okay, so Ness must not have figured out yet that I have a wolf. I know Foster knows because of the whole mate thing. I can feel his wolf, just like he can feel mine. But there is no reason to announce to the rest of the people here that I'm a shifter. Wondering why I elected to withhold this information? Simple, I'm rogue, and pack wolves have no use for rogue wolves.

"Tell me, gorgeous, were we so boring you decided to split right after you got there?" Finch asks as he pops a fry into his mouth before giving a little wink. Lindsey is smiling at me, but I don't miss her eyes flicking towards Foster every couple of seconds. While the man himself doesn't bother to look in my direction. My mere presence is enough to piss him off since his jaw is clenched tight if the constant ticking of it since Finch spoke is anything to go by.

"Sorry, I'm not much of a party person."

"Next time, make sure you give me at least one beer before you decide to bugger out." Finch wiggles his eyebrows.

"I don't think there will be—"I don't get the rest of my sentence out before Foster interrupts me.

"Are you all ready to play darts or what? We can play a round or two and then head back to my place."

"Shay?" Finch asks in a questioning manner. Right now, I am not sure if he is asking if I want to play or go back to Fosters with them; hell, I can't say what he's asking, but regardless, the answer is....

"No." "No!" Foster and my response is spoken simultaneously, although he gives his response with much more force than mine.

"I thought you had to work tomorrow, Foss?" Ness asks as I make my way back to the bar. I hear Foster's response just before I am out of earshot.

"I do, but Fincher here will be at my place cleaning up the mess left by everyone on Saturday."

For the next two hours, I feel like I'm walking on eggshells while Foster and Finch teach Ness and Linds how to play darts. On the other hand, Mandy looks like she is ready to knock the piss out of Lindsey every time she asks for help.

13

I try to keep my eyes directed anywhere other than where they are; however, the few times I do glance at them, I admit seeing Foster with his hands on Lindsey's hips as he corrects her stance has my wolf whimpering.

I know this is hard on you. I'm really sorry you have to go through this after everything else you have suffered. We're strong enough to ignore whatever this is we are feeling. Remember, we were able to do it with Brady. I silently try to reassure her.

Brady was not our mate. He is our mate, and I long to run with his wolf. He calls to me when we are this close. It breaks my heart to know she is suffering. I would do almost anything to stop her anguish.

Can we talk to him? She asks in response to my thought while I think anything but that.

Episode Thirty: Discovery

Foster

THE SECOND I realized she had left, I wanted nothing more than to go after her and bring her back to my cottage or, at the very least, make sure she got safely back to her place. Which apparently is Seamus's old house.

I hate how I treated her. Not to mention Shadow has gone silent since the whole interaction.

Lindsey also now seems to hold out some hope something may happen between us, further cementing my asshole of the year status.

Of the year try from this decade. No, better yet, this century. Yeah, that fits you better, asshole of the century. Of course, the first time Shadow talks to me in days is to insult me.

Thanks.

Just keepin' it real, asshole. He snarls.

Marcelle Valentine

So nice to hear from you again. But he has fallen silent once more.

Even I have to admit he's right; if I keep digging this hole any deeper, I may never find my way out again.

Damn it, how does this girl have my head so twisted up?

No matter how often I declare I want nothing to do with her, the second I am around her, everything flies out the damn window. As a result, my only thought centers on how much I want to spend time with her.

As much as I look forward to this party every year, I want it to end tonight. Lindsey spends half her time sitting next to me and the other half whispering to Ness. I hope my cousin tries to talk some sense into this girl and not encourage her to pursue me. This is what I get for trying to drive a wedge further between Shay and me by pretending something was going on with Lindsey.

Putz! I am, without a doubt, a fucking putz.

Somewhere around three in the morning, my cousins and Lindsey are the only people still here. When Finch goes inside to get some sleep, he announces he found his missing sister; evidently, she passed out on my couch.

This leaves just Lindsey and me standing by the bonfire. I don't know if she was hoping for me to ask her to stay or not. While I don't like the thought of any woman driving by herself at this hour, I'm worried she may read more into it than I am solely looking out for her safety.

Ultimately, the gentleman in me wins out, and I offer her the room I normally sleep in. I can blow up the air mattress and crash upstairs. It may be dusty from the remodel, but there is no way she can misconstrue my intentions this way.

On Sunday, I get up early and go out for a run. Fortunately, by the time I get home, Ness and Lindsey are already gone, leaving the house to Finch and me. My plan today is to work on the upstairs. I only have a few more things to finish up. Once done, I can have Finch help me carry the new bedroom furniture up there before we catch the football game.

Everything is going great until I get a call from Atlas, "Hey, Foss."

"What happened to you last night?"

"I got a lead on what you asked me to look into."

"And?"

"You were right."

"Tell me you were able to find out what they are up to?"

"No, but the shit on the street is there's a new player in the snow biz."

"Is it them?"

"The shit talker definitely, and if I had to guess, the big talker is too, but if you want 100, I can't give you that."

"Thanks for the info. If you hear anything else."

"You'll be the first."

"Thanks." Okay, so Atlas just confirmed Max and Deacon are in bed together, which was no surprise, but what they are doing has my wolf furious. For shit's sake, we have to be extra careful simply because of what we are; now this dumbass Deacon is mixing our pack up with drug running.

I need to get back into his office again. To accomplish this my only option is to find out what his schedule is so I can slip in and out like I did last time. My only saving grace is Ian, his Beta, hates him and will have no issues giving me whatever information I need. I am also acutely aware Ian is probably in the dark regarding his actions. There is no damn way Ian would put the pack in danger.

Ian picks up on the second ring. "Foster, to what do I owe the pleasure?"

"Hey Ian, I was hoping you might be able to help me out with something. Can you tell me if Deacon has any travel plans this week?"

"Yeah, he said something about having to travel to Pueblo tomorrow." That doesn't leave me much time to get in and get out. Unfortunately, I don't have a lot of options here. Since there is nothing I can do until tomorrow, I proceed with my original plan, roping Fin into helping me get my new room set up before we relax with a couple of beers and pizza while we watch the game. While I have never asked Finch to move in, he's over here enough I have started referring to the room he crashes in all the time as his.

The next morning I have to go to the job site to get a few things done before I can snoop around Deacon's office, which works out for the best since I can't imagine the lazy asshole will be up and about this early in the morning.

By the time I finish everything on the site that requires my attention, it's going on twelve o'clock before I get over to Deacon's office. After confirming with Betsy that Deacon hasn't returned yet, I silently slip into his office.

Riffling through every drawer and cupboard in here, I don't find anything that definitively ties Deacon to Max. The only thing I discover is a key and some cryptic correspondence hidden in the false bottom of a drawer in his desk. Before I can scrutinize it, a buzzer goes off, startling the shit out of me until I hear why Betsy is using the intercom.

"Get out, Foster. He's back." Her warning is spoken low, making me realize he is close enough that he would have heard her if her alert had been given any louder. Returning everything to where I found it, I slip out of his office just as he opens the door. Thank goddess Betsy is quick on her feet as she blurts out.

"No problem, Foster. I can ensure we get those supplies ordered and over to the job site ASAP so we can stay on track to finish the job."

"Problem, Foster?" Deacon eyes me suspiciously.

"Not anymore, thanks to Betsy." When he continues to glare from me to her, I add, "We were short on some of the electrical supplies we needed to finish the Whitmore job, but she found what we need so we won't fall off schedule. She's a gem."

"Yes…. A real peach." I'm unsure if his clipped answer is him just being the typical asshole he is with me or if he suspects something. I guess I will have to figure out what he's up to without further involving Betsy.

Once he has shut the door, I mouth a silent Thank you, which grants me one of Betsy's that was way too close smiles before I leave.

A new text message from Ness has me groaning since I completely forgot I promised to meet her and Lindsey at Stooges to teach them how to play darts tonight. I contemplate making up just about any excuse in the world to get me out of it, but in the end, I know Ness well enough to understand she will just hound me to death until I relent and give in to her request.

After I respond with a quick 'on the way,' she returns with a smiling emoji before advising me they are ordering burgers for all of us, so I better hurry.

I am not overly enthused with the thought of Lindsey reading more into this than me simply not being able to tell my cousin no, yet worse than worrying about how Lindsey will see this is the thought of Shay being there. I can deal with the Lindsey issues, but the Shay one is becoming increasingly more difficult each time I'm around her.

When I arrive at Stooge's, it seems the moon goddess has taken pity on this fool since I don't see Shay anywhere in the bar. Letting some of the tension in my shoulders relax for the first time since Ness sent the text.

Par for the course, the only available chair at their table is next to Lindsey. I recognize I now have no choice but to have a candid conversation with Linds; however, before I do, I want to talk with Ness. I don't want her getting pissed off thinking I led her friend on, even though I guess this is precisely what I did, so I deserve Ness's ire.

"Ha, I told you he would come," Ness laughs as she pokes Fin in the chest. In turn, he dramatically rolls his eyes at me.

"You just cost me a ten spot."

"You're the dumbass who bet your sister I wouldn't come. Serves you right since you know I can never—"

"Tell me no," Ness interrupts with a cackling laugh meant to mirror that of a wicked witch. She even wiggles her fingers like she is casting a spell in my direction. Which has Finch and me laughing with her.

"Hi, Foster," Lindsey sheepishly interjects as soon as we manage to get our fits of laughter under control.

"Hey, Linds."

Shay, Shadow roars before I feel her moving towards us. The tension that previously slipped away is back in full force as I sense her approaching. Trying to keep Shadow in check, I miss most of their conversation until I hear my cousin calling her gorgeous, which has Shadow growling. I can't say anything to him, and I know if he realized who she was, he would never speak to her like this, but since I have no intention of claiming her, I also have no intention of telling my cousin who she is to me.

"Next time, make sure you give me at least one beer before you decide to bugger out." If my cousin doesn't stop flirting with her, I'm going to fucking kick his ass.

"I don't think there will be—" Shadow slams against my restraints, and I know I need to put some distance between us if I have any hope of reigning him back in, which is why I continue with my dick of the day attitude and interrupt her.

"Are you all ready to play darts or what? We can play a round or two and then head back to my place." Why did I have to add the 'my place' part?

"Shay?" There is no god damn way Finch just invited her back to my cottage. I know he finds her attractive, and the thought of him hitting on her, especially in my god damn house, is enough to send me into a frenzy.

"No." "No!" Thankfully, she's in agreement with me on this.

"I thought you had to work tomorrow, Foss?"

"I do, but Fincher here will be at my place cleaning up the mess left by everyone on Saturday." Since my cousin is so damn interested in picking something up, he can start with the mess left at my place while leaving my mate out of it.

My mate?

Fuck, when did Shay go from this girl to my mate? I am so fucked if I don't figure something out soon.

Episode Thirty-One: Surprise

Shay

 $\mathcal{M}$ Y WALK HOME from the bar last night was extremely uncomfortable because of my lack of a coat. As hopeful as I was that I wouldn't need one, my short trek home proved how wrong I was, which is why I now find myself traveling out to Foster's place to get the one I left in my rush to get out of there the night of his party.

Thankfully, Hyde offered to give me a ride leaving me confident I could get in and get out before he returned home from work. I may have overheard him saying he would be at work today, but Finch would be there cleaning up the mess.

With one issue potentially resolved, I now face my next, figuring out how I can convince Hyde to drop me off in the middle of nowhere and leave me there. I may have accepted the ride, but I cannot let him go onto pack lands.

Taking a non-shifter on pack land without the Alpha's permission is a huge no-no. Hell, as a rogue, I shouldn't be going here without a pack member bringing me. If I'm caught, I could face losing so much more than just a stupid coat; I could lose my life. The pack would be well within their rights to attack me on sight.

If I had any extra money to replace the one I left, I sure as hell wouldn't be risking my neck coming after the one in his house. My only saving grace is Foster's place is not in the heart of pack land; it sits on the outskirts. So fingers crossed, I can get in and get out before I alert any of his pack mates to my presence.

As long as I don't shift, they won't be able to sense me, but it won't stop them from attacking me if they think I am a threat to the pack. With the gate pulled across the road, there is no way he can offer to drive me any further, which seems to be the only blessing I will receive today. I know there is no way in hell I could persuade him to leave me if it wasn't.

As suspected, it took me thirty minutes of constant reassurance I would be fine to convince Hyde to leave me in the middle of nowhere. He went as far as to offer to wait by the side of the road regardless of how long I planned to visit with my friend, which is the excuse I gave him to explain why I was coming out here.

I only stay on the dirt road long enough to confirm Hyde has driven away before I slip into the cover offered by the thick trees. It's not much if the pack has their scouts out, but it is better than marching straight down the middle of the road.

I arrive at his house just before 1:30. My heart sinks a little when I discover everything is already cleaned up. The house

23

appears to be locked up tight, and Finch is nowhere to be seen. Man, I hope I didn't miss him.

As I knock lightly on the door, my only thought is, here's hoping he's still inside. When the door flies open, my heart sinks when I discover Foster, not Finch, standing there.

"Ah…. Wha—….. What are you doing here?" I stammer.

"I live here." The sound of his deep baritone voice swirls inside me and settles like a building heat deep in my core. "What are you doing here?"

"Ah…. Well…. I," I mutter before blurting, "my mistake." Turning, I sprint down the three steps to his yard, thinking that freezing is preferential to facing this man who obviously hates me. It's not that cold today. If the only time of day I really need to worry about this issue is at night when I walk home from Stooges, I can wear two or three sweatshirts. Yeah, that's the answer to this problem. Geesh, why didn't I think of this earlier?

"Hey," Foster yells as he grabs my arm.

"Don't touch me," I shout as I whip back in his direction. Foster raises his hand as he takes a step away from me. Heat flares across my cheeks, realizing I just made a total ass out of myself. It's not like this guy plans to hurt me as Travis did. Hell, he can't stand to be near me, let alone touch me. Resulting in me quickly mumbling, "Sorry."

"No need to apologize. It was my mistake, not yours." I nod my head before dropping my eyes towards the ground. "Now, why don't you tell me why you came all the way out to my house?"

"I forgot something here." The timid sound of my voice is something I hate. I can't stand that I am allowing anyone to have this level of control over me.

"Which is?"

24

"My coat."

"Wait, you've been without a coat since the party?"

"Yeah." I quietly confirm as I prepare myself for the inevitable lecture I know is coming about how stupid, irresponsible, and careless I am.

"Shay..." He knows my name; I'm shocked. Not to mention, I don't think I have ever heard my name sound as wonderful as it does when spoken from the lips I am entirely too focused on right now. "...you should have called Ness. She could have brought it to you."

"I couldn't." Suddenly embarrassed by my lack of money and inability to buy something everyone else seems to take for granted; a phone.

"Let me guess, Ness forgot to give you her number? Why does that not surprise me? My cousin is great, but she can be a scatterbrain regarding minor details like this."

Unlike all the times I have been chastised throughout my life, I realize his words are not meant to belittle Ness; they are lighthearted and spoken with love. Even so, I can't let him think Ness didn't give me her number because she did. I didn't keep it since I had no way of calling her. The thought of telling him my financial situation is mortifying, but I won't let him think this is Ness's issue.

"No, it's not like that. I.... I don't have a phone."

"Really?" Thankfully, he must recognize I am uncomfortable, so he does not press the issue. When he turns back towards his house without saying anything, I take it as my cue to leave. This is until he calls out. "Where are you going?"

"Home?" I say questioningly.

"Shay, come in and get your coat," he snaps before adding, "although I have to say I don't recall seeing any abandoned

25

clothes lying around." I can't tell if it irritated him because I just showed up at his house unannounced and uninvited or not.

The wind picks up, causing a shiver to rip through me. A quick glance at the sky reveals the looming storm has arrived sooner than predicted. If I hurry, maybe I can grab my coat and streak back through the woods. With any luck, I can get most of the way home before this storm hits.

Reluctant to enter his house, I end up standing here looking like a scared and timid little girl, and since I vowed I would never let anyone put me in that role again, I square my shoulders as I follow him into his place.

Oh my Goddess, it's not here. This is the one prevailing thought I have as he searches his entire house and doesn't find it. This guy is going to think I lied just so I could get close to him; I feel like an idiot. I know I didn't grab it before I left that night. Shortly after I took off, I realized I had forgotten it. I also distinctly remember having it when I was carrying the beer into his house because it got caught on the door handle, causing me to almost drop the alcohol.

After we searched every square inch of his house, he called Ness only to find out she saw my coat lying there and took it with her to give to me the next time she saw me but had forgotten about it until now.

Well, that's just fucking grand. I could have avoided this entire awkward situation had she just returned it to me last night when she saw me. Yet I have no one to blame since she did stop over at the house Sunday and probably would have given it to me then if I hadn't pretended like I wasn't home like some chickenshit coward.

Muttering a half-hearted red-faced apology, I turn to leave, only to be greeted by the torrent of rain from the storm. Stopping me dead in my tracks.

Episode Thirty-Two: Searching

Brady

WHEN I ARRIVE back at the pack house, the first thing I see is Ophelia and Rose, who appear to be in the middle of a heated conversation. Neither of these two is on my list, so I feel no need to immerse myself in their argument.

As I mount the stairs, I hear Ophelia snap, "I have to tell him, Rosey, we should have said something a long time ago. Hell, we should have spoken up that night. We need to do the right thing."

"But, Fee—"

"No, Rosey, if we continue to stay quiet, then we're no better than the rest of them, and I would like to think we're not assholes. Brady, I need to talk to you."

"Can it wait until—"

"No, it can't." Ophelia's determination has me questioning what is so urgent. Nodding my head, she looks over her shoulder at Rose, who doesn't seem to agree with whatever

Ophelia plans on telling me. Closing the door to my office, I offer a seat to Ophelia. I patiently wait as she sorts out whatever it is she is so desperate to tell me.

"Can I ask you something, Brady? Something I need an honest answer to."

"Sure."

"Do you agree with how the Alpha and Luna have been running this pack, specifically how they treat some of our pack members?"

Not understanding where she is going with this line of questions or if this is some kind of test from my father, making my responses more cautious than I would like, "I believe my father and mother do what they think is best."

"That was a very diplomatic response, but I don't care about your beliefs. I am asking you if you think what they do is right. Because I have got to be honest with you, Brady, I don't."

"Was there something or someone, in particular, you are referring to?"

"Shay. Do you think what they did to Shay, how they treated her? Do you think it was right?"

"No, I don't. And if I'm being honest, Fee, I don't think any of us treated her right," it's the first time I think I have ever fully given voice regarding my thoughts on how not just mom and dad treated one of our pack members but all of us. Ophelia and Rose included.

"I agree. We all should have done more for Shay. That's why I'm here now, hoping to do better for her." Ophelia's eyes are closed as she takes a deep breath. When she releases it, she opens her eyes and begins telling me what she came to say.

"Shay didn't steal Natashia's necklace; if I had to guess, she didn't take the money either."

"Why do you think she's innocent? Do you have any proof to substantiate your claims?"

"When has anyone ever needed proof to voice a suspicion in this pack? It certainly wasn't needed the night Shay was accused." I must admit she has a point there. Regardless, I am unwilling to chase a white rabbit down the hole to the land of make-believe on nothing more than assumptions and speculation. It doesn't matter that I already have my own misgivings; I need Ophelia to give me something to help me prove her innocence.

"During the time the stupid necklace supposedly came up missing, Shay was with Rose and me."

"Why wouldn't Shay just say that when my mom questioned her?"

"She was trying to protect Rose and me."

"Protect you from what?"

Ophelia swallows hard before she blurts out, "Your father. She was trying to protect us from your father finding out Rose and I are a couple. I love Rose, and she loves me, but your father will never accept us not doing our part in increasing the pack size by having our own pups."

*****

At this point, I don't really care who sees me entering Natashia's room because if I find any proof she has been lying to me, she will not like the consequences of her actions.

If anyone else has been involved with her deception, then they will be in the same shit river as Tosh, and I don't give a rat's ass who it is. After everything I learned while in Whitefish and from Ophelia, I know Shay wasn't involved in taking the money; I need to find irrefutable proof to show my father.

Riffling through the contents of her room, I find definitive proof she's been lying. What I discovered does not link her to the missing money, but if she lied about this, it is possible she has not been entirely forthcoming regarding the allegations against Shay. I do not know why Natashia has had it out for Shay this entire time, but I intend to find out. After I checked the rest of her room, I moved to the next room on my list; Sadie's.

Unlike Natashia's room, I find nothing in Sadie's to indicate any involvement on her part, even though I have little doubt she is not innocent since Natashia doesn't do anything without her sidekick Sadie. I am not done with my quest for the truth, so I go to the next room I intend to rip apart; the man who sounded the alarm the night she took off and one of my best friends, Travis.

Having checked everywhere else, the last place to search is the closet, but I no sooner open the door than Travis strolls in.

"Brady?"

Needing to think of anything I can give him to explain why I am in his room searching through his shit, I blurt out, "Did you take my black sweatshirt?"

"Damn, man, I just borrowed it. I was going to give it back." How in the hell did I manage to ask about the one thing he just so happened to have of mine? Without my permission, I might add.

He walks past me, reaches in, grabs my shirt, and closes the door concealing the interior from my view the entire time. Almost like he doesn't want me to see whatever he has inside of there.

I figure as soon as I question Natashia about what I found in her room, the cat will most definitely be out of the bag. Unless I can come up with a damn good excuse about how this little piece of evidence ended up in my possession without drawing attention to my investigation. Or unless I bring him in on it without revealing how I discovered her lie.

Scrubbing my hand down my face, I sigh, knowing he will not be able to resist questioning what my issue is. "What's the matter with you lately?"

Bingo, there's my in. "Sorry, man, I'm just a little off today."

"So I noticed. Why don't you tell me what's got you so rattled?"

"Someone told me they saw the necklace Tosh accused Shay of stealing in her room, and before you ask who it was, just know I promised them they could stay anonymous."

"Didn't your mom get it back from Shay?"

"No. Shay denied knowing anything about it. As far as I know, she never changed her tune."

"So, what are you thinking?"

"I don't know. I plan to ask her why she would make something like this shit up, though."

"You want me to be there when you question her?"

"Nope, I think if we're both there, she's gonna refuse to say anything, but thanks for offering." Something flicks through his eyes briefly before he shrugs and flops on his bed. Taking this as my cue to leave, I stroll out of his room.

Imagine my surprise when I discover Natashia chatting with Sadie and Maggie in the hallway. The look flashing across Maggie's face tells me everything I need to know: I'm on the right track.

Episode Thirty-Three: Giving In

Foster

*D*ON'T LET OUR *mate go, asshole.* This is the first time Shadow has said anything to me since the night I chased her away. I can tell she is preparing to leave, but since I didn't hear a car pull up, I have to assume if she doesn't have a phone, she doesn't have a car either.

I know I could take her home, but I admit I have missed my furball friend, so if spending some time with her today will make him happy, I can deal with it for one day.

Yeah, you keep telling yourself that, asshole. Maybe it might be true one day, or you could just admit you want to be around her as much as I do, Shadow growls.

Keep it up, and I will show you how wrong you are, I retort.

"Shay, you can't leave right now. It's pouring down rain."

"It's not that bad," she tries to reason.

When I stroll over to the door, I am so close her scent is overwhelming every one of my senses. My pathetic attempt to ignore how great she smells is to look out the screen door. I realize the rain is coming down so hard out there I can't see the swing on the other side of the yard; as a result, I can't help the little chuckle escaping me when I glance down at her.

"Yeah, it's nothing more than a light rain, actually closer to a sprinkle. No way will it soak you through within thirty seconds. My mistake."

"I don't want to be a bother. I can wait out on the porch. That is if you don't mind."

"Do you really think I'm that much of an asshole I would make you sit outside in this damp, chilly weather?"

"I never…. I didn't mean…. I'm—" Deciding to let her off easy, I pull the chair out at my table before I throw the leftover pizza in the oven to heat it up.

Having lunch with Shay finally calms Shadow, and I decide to take this opportunity to try to learn more about her. I can't believe this girl has been a rogue her whole life. I also don't miss how jumpy she is, so if she was in a pack, I can't imagine it was a good experience.

Hell, I know firsthand the pack Alpha is not always the best choice since I had to put one down and may need to do it with the asshole who took over for him. I decided to dive into my questions because something told me if I beat around the bush, it would put her on guard faster than just being straight.

"Where are you from?"

"Ummm." Shay shifts uncomfortably, so I remain quiet until she answers. "Montana."

"Is that where your pack is located?"

"I don't have a pack."

34

"Shay, you may be rogue now, but you haven't always been. Did something happen to your pack or to you?" When I ask this last part, her eyes drop to her plate. So something happened to her. I've heard tales of some packs forcing their female members into a relationship. I wonder if this is what happened to her, and I have to be honest, the thought not only has Shadow growling but fury building in me. "So the answer to my question is you. Something happened to you to make you leave your pack."

"I should really get going."

"Shay, it's still pouring outside. We don't have to discuss your old pack if you are uncomfortable. Why don't you tell me something about yourself? Something you're okay with sharing."

"I like to cook." She tells me as her eyes shift around my kitchen.

"Imagine that. I like to eat." This grants me a small smile from her. I admit I like it when she smiles.

"Apparently, cold pizza and burgers from Stooge's are your staples."

"I don't have much time to cook. Besides, I don't like to cook."

"With a kitchen like this, how could you not?" Her face lights up as she stands to further inspect the appliances. I remain quiet as she wanders around, skimming her fingers over the surfaces. An image of her wearing one of my shirts as we cook breakfast together floods my thoughts. Where the hell did that shit come from? If I could smack myself, I would.

"So, you like to cook, you're a pretty," her head snaps towards me, hearing me use the word pretty, and for a brief period, I contemplate leaving my thought with this. Still, if I want to keep this whole no-mate declaration in place, I need to elaborate on what I just said and moving forward, I need to think before I speak. "adept dart player. You were able to charm your way into the heart of the gruff and grumpy Seamus, not to mention Hyde and Jerry seem smitten with you. What else?"

"Nope, it's your turn. Tell me something about you."

"Finch and Ness are my cousins, but in reality, I view them more as siblings than cousins."

"It must be great to have a bond like this with someone else, but I've got to tell you, it's not really that much of a revelation."

"Alrighty, smarty pants, do you know why I'm so close to them then?" Shay shakes her head as she returns to the table and takes the chair next to mine. "I'm so close to them because my aunt raised me."

"Are your parents...." I imagine she wants to inquire if they're dead, but she doesn't have the heart to ask.

"My mom passed away when I was very young. It's been so long that I have forgotten more about her than I remember. I never knew my dad. He's just some asshole who broke my mom's heart and left her to raise me alone. My aunt got custody of me right after my mom died."

"Sounds like your aunt is a special lady."

"She's the best. Your turn. Tell me something else about you."

"My favorite time to.... You know.... Go out for a run...."

"You mean to release your wolf? It's okay; you can talk about your wolf here. Shifting is a part of our existence, Shay."

"My favorite time to run with her is first thing in the morning when the grass is still heavy with dew, and the air is still fresh from the start of a new day. I love watching the sunrise."

"Mine is at night when my senses are heightened, and the nocturnal animals are chasing their prey." Her smile brightens her entire face. Shadow pushes forward, begging me for some time with her wolf. "I'm going out for a run; wanna come?"

"What, like right now?"

"Yeah, the rain has slowed to a drizzle, and the sun should be back out before long. Come for a run with me."

"Won't Lindsey be upset if she finds out about this?" And there it is, pretending there was anything between Lindsey and me has just come back to bite me in the ass. I need to set this straight right now.

"Why would Linds be upset?"

"Because I thought…. She's your…."

"Girlfriend?"

"Yeah." Shay tucks a strand of loose hair behind her ear as she looks down at her hands folded on her lap.

"Lindsey is not my girlfriend. She is Ness's best friend, but that's it. So what do you say? Wanna let your wolf loose and come out to play with me?"

"I've never actually run with another wolf before."

"You didn't go out for runs with your previous pack?"

"I was not…. My pack…. You know what, it doesn't matter."

"Well, you are welcome to join me if you want."

Without hesitation, I slip my shirt off before kicking off my shoes. I admit knowing her eyes are roaming over my body is a turn-on, but when I unbutton my jeans, I realize she was not prepared to see any more of it. At least if the color of her skin is any clue. Her face turns bright red as she swiftly drops her gaze to the ground.

"Are you coming, or are you planning on continuing to stare at me while I take off my clothes?"

"Oh Goddess, I'm so sorry."

"Don't apologize; it really isn't that big of a deal." I begin to tell her until I see an opportunity to spend more time with her, especially since Shadow is desperately pleading for her to join us. "No, wait. On second thought, you can make it up to me by coming out for a run."

She goes quiet for a long time as she chews on her bottom lip, looking out towards the woods. I can tell she's torn between coming with me and possibly telling me to go fuck myself. I can't say I blame her since I have been such a royal asshole to her since the first time we saw one another. I would be lying if I didn't admit to hoping she agrees to come, but either way, it's her choice. The only thing I can do is wait and hope she joins me. The ball is in Shay's court now.

"Would you mind turning around so I can? Umm...."

"Take off your clothes." I have never been around another shifter who isn't willing to strip down to release their wolf before, lending truth to her previous confession she never ran with another wolf. "If it would make you more comfortable, I can shift and wait for you around the side of the cottage."

"Yeah, okay."

Episode Thirty-Four: Shifting

Shay

$\mathcal{B}$EING THIS CLOSE to him and spending time with him has been like finding a missing piece of myself. I never realized how wonderful it could be to romp through the woods with someone else.

The first time Foster's wolf dove on mine, she didn't know how to respond, but when he started jumping around in front of us, I immediately reassured her what he was doing.

He's trying to play with you.

Sneaking up behind them, my wolf leaps on his back, nipping at his ear. His wolf is strong and easily flips mine onto our back. As he stands over us, I fully expect him to go in for the kill. I would have, but instead of latching down on our throat, he runs his muzzle against hers. The sensation sends waves of excitement rushing through not just my wolf but me as well.

When I look up, I find the same amber eyes with golden flecks as Foster's staring back at me. His black fur is shiny and feels like silk. I have never actually seen my wolf, so aside from my white paws and legs, I don't know what she looks like. I can tell you that Foster's wolf is beautiful, magnificent, and stronger than any other wolf I have ever seen before.

We continue playing until a low growl announces the approach of a predator, and not just any predator, a huge black bear. This is the first time I have ever encountered something like this, possibly due to my lack of traveling in this form. Foster's wolf does not hesitate as he returns the warning with one of his own, placing himself between the bear and my wolf.

When the bear continues towards us, I move next to him. If one of us intimidated the bear, let's see what he does against two. My wolf instinctually knows what to do as she drops her head, growling and snapping at the air in front of us. The bear makes the wise decision to turn the other way. Once he's gone, Foster's wolf immediately turns back to us, rubbing his face against ours. On the return trip to his house, I notice his wolf doesn't wander far from us.

When we arrive at his house, Foster shifts back, but I'm not as comfortable even though he has proven himself to be nothing short of a gentleman today. After pulling his pants on, he grabs my clothes and heads inside. When I linger in the yard, he pokes his head back out the door, asking, "You coming?"

I follow him into the house; he takes my clothes and puts them on a bed before softly saying, "I'll just give you some privacy."

The smell of food cooking has my stomach growling as I put my clothes back on. I glance at the clock on the wall, knowing I only have an hour before I have to be at work, so if I hope to make it, I need to leave now. I can wait to eat until after work; it won't be the first time I have gone hungry.

Pulling my hair up in a ponytail, I walk out, not knowing which Foster I will find when I leave this room. Will it be the Foster from previous interactions, or will it be the man I met today?

When I walk out and find him in the kitchen cooking, I cannot help but feel the pull of our mate bond.

"I thought you said you didn't know how to cook?"

"I said I didn't like to cook; I never said I didn't know how to do it."

Smiling at him, I start toward the door until he asks, "You're really going to leave after I've been sweating my ass off to make us something to eat?"

"I kinda figured you probably had enough of me by now." His face shifts and I'm unsure if what I see is good or bad. "Besides, I need to get back if I hope to make it to work on time."

"What time do you need to be there?"

"Six."

"Okay, so plenty of time. Have a seat, enjoy your meal, and I'll drive you to work. I'm going there anyway for the tournament."

The dinner starts out awkward since I'm unsure what to say to him, but in the end, I say the only thing that matters, "Thanks for today. I had a lot of fun. My wolf has never been able to do that before. I don't think she has ever been so happy."

"Shadow is quiet for the first time," he hesitates before saying, "in weeks."

"Whose Shadow?"

"My wolf, what's your wolf's name?"

Swallowing, I realize I am about to show my lack of knowledge. "She doesn't have a name."

"Your pack never had a naming ceremony for you after your first shift?"

"No," I feel like such an idiot; why did he have to be the one to ask me this? While I would have felt stupid admitting this to Ness, at least I wouldn't feel like a complete idiot. And why didn't Maggie ever say anything to me about this? "My pack.... They didn't...."

"It's okay. You talk with her, don't you?"

"Yes, all the time."

"Does she have a name she feels belongs to her?"

"How would I know?"

"Ask her."

No, Shay, that part of me was suppressed for too long. I have no idea what name you would call me. Her quiet confession is said in a way I know she is aware I will blame myself for this too, but she doesn't want me to. It doesn't matter because I hate what I have done to her.

Don't be sad, Shay.

Did you know you were supposed to have a name?

Yes, but your life was much too complicated back then to worry about such trivial matters.

Your name is not a trivial matter. I shift uncomfortably in my chair, feeling my heart again aching because I let her down.

"Shay, you don't have to name her today. If you both are unsure, think about it before choosing one. Have you ever even seen your wolf?" I shake my head. "She is smaller than most female wolves, but I imagine this is because you could not exercise her the way she should have been. But she's fast; you had no problem keeping up with me. She is pure white, with a pink nose, but her eyes are the most unusual part of her."

"How so?" I ask as panic rises at the prospect something may be wrong with her, and I never realized it.

"Her eyes are crystal blue, just like yours. I have never witnessed something so amazing or beautiful in my life." I know he wasn't complimenting me; he meant it for my wolf, but I still can't help the warm feeling pooling low in my belly. I have to say that for someone who doesn't like to cook, Foster is pretty amazing at it.

True to his word, he drove me to work as soon as we finished eating. This guy shocks the shit out of me because I remember someone once saying he works construction, but his truck, just like his house, is spotless. I almost ask if I should take my shoes off so I don't muck up the interior.

When I stand there refusing to get in, he finally advises, "I'm fine with staying home tonight, but Seamus might get mad if he's short a waitress."

"I know."

"Generally, in order to receive a ride, you need to get into the vehicle, Shay."

"I know."

"Do you need help? If you do, I'd be happy to give you a boost."

Snapping me out of my stupor, I climb into his truck with Foster's booming laugh filling the cab.

When I get to work, Foster joins Finch, Ness, Lindsey, Atlas, and Denver while I hustle my ass behind the bar. Hyde has several questions about who I went to see, how long I was there, and if I got what I needed. While Mandy eyes me suspiciously, she must have seen me come into the bar, followed closely by Foster. So right now, she's giving me all the shit work while keeping me as far away from his table as possible.

The worst is the one I am currently tasked with; my skin crawls when I realize who she is making me take these drinks to. The way Max and his goons eye me, you would think I am the last drink of water in a desert. Hoping to drop his beers and take my ass behind the bar before they can start anything, my wish is for nothing when Max grabs my ass as I turn to walk away.

"What the fuck do you think you're doing?"

"What? Don't pretend like you are not into me. Everyone in here can see you are."

"I think you're a vile piece of shit. Now take your goddamn hands off me."

Max's expression shifts from flirtatious to rage as he slides to the edge of the booth he has been sitting in. He never releases the painful grip he has on my wrist. Tugging my arm, trying to break it loose, is pointless as he tightens it before yanking me down onto his lap. He emits a low growl as he buries his nose in my hair. The sound warns me he will not accept any further attempt to extricate myself from his embrace.

"Let. Go!" I demand, only to receive a laugh from the men around the table. I glance towards the bar, hoping to find Seamus standing there because I know he will not put up with this, but it's not Seamus who comes to my rescue. It's Foster, and to say I'm mortified would be an understatement.

"She told you to let her go. I suggest you do as the lady asked."

"Aren't you just the white knight, or is it the dark knight?" I'm not sure what this is all about, but Foster loses his cool when he reaches down and wrenches me out of Max's grasp. Max doesn't try to stop him; quite the opposite, he shakes his head at the other men sitting around him when they stand up.

After Foster has me extracted, he leads me out to the parking lot, and this is when I realize the Foster from this afternoon is gone, and the asshole is apparently back.

"I'm not looking for a mate, Shay." He snaps. This is confusing since I neither said anything about being his mate, nor did I ask for his damn help in there.

"Who the hell said anything about us or me wanting a mate?"

"Perfect, so it seems we are on the same damn page." He snarls as he takes a step away from me.

"That it does," I reply as I throw the bar door open, stalking inside.

Episode Thirty-Five: Over It

Shay

I WAS SHOCKED when he started yelling at me the instant he had me outside and pissed when he continued to bitch after I walked back in.

"Next time, keep some distance between you and that asshole. I don't want to make this a thing."

"Nobody god damn asked you to make it a thing," I hiss, throwing my hands up, using air quotes when I repeat his word *thing*. "You did that all on your own."

"Shay."

"You need to get back to your life, and I need to get my ass behind the bar. I'll ensure my problems never bother you again."

"That's not what I—" before Foster can finish, Max interrupts by yelling the stupidest and the furthest thing from reality when it comes to Foster and me.

"Lover's spat?" Max asks loud enough to have the entire bar looking at us.

"We're not friends, let alone lovers!" "Shut the fuck up, asshole." Our answers are snarled simultaneously, but when Foster hears my response about not being friends, his head snaps back in my direction. I'm not sure what the expression he gave me is supposed to mean, but regardless, it doesn't damn well matter. Foster made himself perfectly clear just now. I have no idea why he changed his opinion of me for five hours today. I wish he had remained the same asshole he's been the entire time; maybe my wolf wouldn't be whimpering right now, nor would I have this heavy feeling in my chest.

"Tichy?" Seamus asks as I round the bar, breathing entirely too heavily. I would like to say the reaction is all from being pissed, but it's not. I'm not saying I was looking for a mate; it was just nice being able to talk freely to someone who could tell me the things about being a shifter no one else has ever told me.

The problem is the asshole over there is the only one I have confessed about being a shifter to, so it looks like I got all the information I will be receiving. I am most pissed for my wolf (which, by the way, I will name by tomorrow); she didn't deserve to be introduced to his world only to have it yanked out from under her. Never again. I will never allow anyone to make her feel like this again. I promise you this.

"I'm fine, Seamus."

"Aye, what egit has you so ragin? I'll give 'em the boot."

"It's okay. It was my mistake. One I won't ever make again." I don't know what is worse: the questioning eyes from the people at Foster's table, the amusement coming from Max's,

47

the sympathetic look from Seamus, or the angry glare Mandy is giving me. Fuck my life.

Thankfully, the bar is filling up, keeping me busy enough that I can't sit around thinking about everything that transpired today. I'm doing a pretty good job keeping my mind off everything until I go to retrieve stock and an angry Mandy follows me.

"What the hell happened?"

"Happened with what?"

"Don't play stupid, Shay."

Did I know what she was talking about? Yes. Do I plan to make this easy for her? Hell no.

I have had to deal with enough jealous women to know I should never offer information on what you think they are pissed about; make sure they tell you what has them so upset. This way, you don't dig the hole with them any deeper than necessary. So in answer to her response, I merely shrug my shoulder with the best I have no idea what you are talking about look covering my face.

"You and Foster. What the hell is going on with you and Foster?" Well, at least I can honestly answer this question, even though I am guessing she isn't going to believe me.

"There is absolutely nothing going on between Foster and me. I do not know why he inserted himself into that issue with Max. I certainly never asked him to get involved."

"Did you come with him to work today?" Okay, so this question takes my ability to be honest with her, crumples it up, and tosses it out the damn window. I have to be careful what I say here. I don't want to entirely lie because Foster can dispute it, and so can Hyde. Think, Shay, think.

"We did come in at the same time, yes." Hopefully, she doesn't push this.

"So you came with him?" Of course, this wasn't good enough.

"Aye, I'm not paying ya to be a dosser." Saved by the boss or actually just a momentary reprieve cause I know she is not going to let this go.

"You should know Foster and I have dated before." And there it is. She is staking her claim to a man I'm pretty sure has never so much as given her the time of day. At least not since I've been here, but hey, to each their own. She doesn't have anything to worry about from me. With every declaration I make to distance myself further from Foster, I can feel my wolf retreating further. Which makes me sad. Still, I won't lie to her or leave her hoping for more when there is no hope to be had.

"Cool. I wish you both a long and happy life together." I try to keep any of the hurt or anger I'm feeling from seeping into my response. The last thing I want is to have tension here at work. I can't imagine Seamus would put up with it, and if he has to get rid of someone, I don't imagine the new girl would be the one he keeps.

I keep my distance from Mandy, Max, and especially Foster the rest of the night. It wasn't hard once the tournament was in full swing, and since Mandy asked Ness to hang out when she got off at ten, I knew I wouldn't have to answer her questions tonight. With any luck, perhaps Foster and she will make up, so I don't have to put up with a jealous ex.

My plan for the night is to finish my shift here at Stooges and then release my wolf so we can decide her name. I'm not sure what all is entailed with a naming ceremony, and it doesn't matter because we are going to have our own. I imagine if my previous pack had something like a naming ceremony, it was during the pack runs, which I wasn't permitted to participate in.

So screw all of them; my wolf and I will make our own tradition.

Episode Thirty-Six: Moon

Foster

I SHOULD HAVE never invited Shay in when she showed up. I should have kept my distance. Initially, I admit she got past my front door only because of Shadow's constant begging. My problem is the longer she was around us, the more I wanted to spend time with her. Damn it, I can feel all the walls I built up being pulled down: one smile, one laugh, one shy look at a time.

The minor details she gave me revealed so much about her previous life, yet left me wanting to learn more. I know her pack didn't treat her like they should have, as evident since her wolf never received her name, Shay's timidness about shifting in front of me, and her overall lack of knowledge about pack life. I know she's rogue, but knowing the little bit I do about her, I don't blame Shay for choosing the path she took.

The instant Shadow saw her wolf, his interest grew from merely wanting to be near our mate to his desperate desire to claim her and have her claim him. I also know that the white wolf we discovered lying next to the stream was Shay.

If she had not needed to come to work, I could have happily spent the rest of the night getting to know her. Not to mention getting lost in those beautiful blue eyes. Instead, I'm sitting here trying to keep my eyes directed at my fingers drumming the table. The most unfortunate part of this whole thing is Mandy witnessed us coming in together, so now she is treating Shay like shit.

As much as I want to march over there and tell Mandy to lay the fuck off of her, I stay where I am because I know anything I say or do will only make it worse for Shay. That is until I hear Shay growling to let her go. When I look up and find her on Max's lap, I cannot contain the fury racing through me as my wolf wants nothing more than to rip this asshole apart.

Storming over, I confront Max; as I release enough of my wolf, I know my eyes are shining much brighter than mortals would. Max realizes how close I am to losing it and wisely decides to release her.

My next action proves how twisted she has me because instead of walking back over to my table, I pull her outside. Knowing I need a reason why I drug her out here instead of just asking if she's okay, I yell at her. I couldn't be a bigger asshole if I tried, and now I feel like we are further apart than ever. The problem is I no longer want to keep her at a distance.

When Max yells something about lovers when we come back inside, the reality of how badly I just screwed up hits me like a ton of bricks when she responds we are not friends. Damn, hearing her say this hurts more than I care to admit.

As soon as the pool tournament is over, I don't waste any time getting out of there, but not before I tell Ness, under no uncertain terms, is she to bring Mandy out to my place. I know I pissed her off since Finch and I had plans to go back there after the tournament. But since Ness has both Lindsey and now Mandy, I don't need that headache.

Little did I know how important this declaration would be.

*****

Shay

I didn't get out of the bar until close to two in the morning. Still, I made my wolf a promise, which I intend to keep. I jog home to drop off my stuff before I shift and take off into the woods. Running through the woods this time doesn't give me the same sort of peace I have previously felt, and it really doesn't give me the same enjoyment I had today with Foster and Shadow.

No matter. Tonight is about finding my wolf's name, making sure she loves it, and declaring it to the Moon Goddess. I let her run for a while, and she takes us straight to the rocky outcrop by the *stream.*

What are you thinking?

I have never had a name, Shay. I'm unsure if tradition dictates I am supposed to tell you what I like or if you are just supposed to pick for me.

Fuck tradition. We're doing this our way.

Well then, I would like you to pick my name for me.

I contemplate it for several minutes before I believe I have come up with the perfect name. I only hope she likes it as much as I do. *Moon.*

Moon?

It was you who kept me going. You are the guiding light I seek to follow; through your dreams, I have found peace and am never alone because of you and the beauty you emit.

I love it.

Moon and I lay by the stream enjoying the frosty night air. The only thing that would have made this night better would be if Shadow…. Nope, not going there. Absolutely not. If I could have Shadow here without Foster, I would happily have him here for Moon's sake, but this isn't an option.

Our peaceful night is interrupted when I hear a low growl behind us. Moon leaps to her feet as we try to figure out where the sound came from. It does not leave us wondering for long as a large rust-colored wolf rushes out of the brush not twenty yards away from where we are standing.

Instinct kicks in as Moon bolts across the stream, heading further into pack land with the larger wolf hot on my trail. I know we are taking an extreme risk going this way, but I have no choice because I can't go back. I just pray if they have their sentries or scouts out patrolling, they are far enough away it will prevent this wolf from mind-linking with them because if he does, we're fucked.

Moon is pushing herself harder than she ever has before. If something drastic doesn't happen soon, the angry wolf behind me will be on us before we make it much further.

Shay, he's gaining.

Just run, Moon. Run!

The wolf is close enough to hear him inhaling each breath between the snapping of his jaws. The dangerous-looking fangs he is hell-bent on burying deep within us are on full display.

Shay!

Change directions NOW, Moon.

She turns just as he leaps. Had we not done this, we would be under the other wolf. Judging by the size and bulk, I would say it is male. I do not know how I will get out of this mess, but I know Moon can't keep up this pace much longer.

Thankfully, when he leapt, we switched directions, causing him to slam headfirst into a tree, momentarily stunning him. This allowed Moon to put some distance between them and us. When Moon rounds the next corner, I recognize the area at the same time she does. We were here earlier today, and as a result, we know where we need to go. Making our desperate plea escape us in unison….

Foster! Shadow!

Episode Thirty-Seven: Challenge

Foster

FINCH IS AWARE I have been looking into Deacon's activities, and it is high time I clue him in on everything I have discovered thus far. It is only fair since Deacon's actions will affect all of us, not just me.

"Finn, I need to tell you something."

After finishing the beer he chugged, he responded first with a burp before a gurgled, "What's up?"

"You okay?" I ask with a laugh.

"Golden." Which is his typical response when he wants to say everything is great.

"This is a serious conversation we need to have." Finch sits up, showing I have his full attention. No matter how much he likes to clown around, he knows how significant this is when he hears my tone.

"I want you to know that I looked into Deacon after Ian asked me to, and I found something disturbing. Deacon and Maximus are working together. I discovered they are using our pack lands and Max's transport company to move drugs into the area."

"Are you sure about this? I mean, Deacon is a lot of things, but by putting our pack in danger. He would be exposing himself too."

"I found a check made out to Max's company; he has had several meetings with Max, but the most damning evidence came from Atlas after I asked him to look into it. He confirmed they are definitely running drugs."

"Son of a bitch. That asshole is going to bring down the entire pack doing this shit. I never trusted that fucker. He's too sleazy to be an Alpha; he has always only been out for what is best for him. So what are we going to do about this?"

"*We* aren't doing shit. I need you to stay out of it in case my plan doesn't work out. You have to be beyond reproach. I need to know someone will still be around to stop him."

"What the hell are you going to do, Foss?" I know Finch doesn't really need me to tell him what I am planning, but if he needs to hear me say it, then so be it.

"I'm going to challenge him for pack alpha."

*****

Shay

Sprinting across the field, the one we romped through not even twenty-four hours ago with Shadow and Foster, I can't help but think how close we are to salvation. Even if Foster has already made it clear he doesn't want to bail me out of trouble, I can't imagine he would turn us away knowing we are in danger. Besides, it's not like he would actually have to fight; the only thing he would need to do is tell his pack mates who I am to save my life.

We only make it midway across when the other wolf leaps, digging its claws into Moon's rump. We cannot help the howls of pain filling the space around us. Why in the hell did I keep pushing my luck coming this close to pack land? I have no one to blame for the circumstances I find myself in.

Moon kicks her back legs out, dislodging him and knocking him to the ground. Using this as an opportunity to put some more space between us, Moon picks up her pace. The searing pain from his attack isn't helping her keep up the speed we need to maintain distance between us and our pursuer. The most frustrating part is I can't help her because I wouldn't stand a chance against him.

This time when he attacks, he uses his entire body to knock us off our feet. The impact sends us all slamming to the ground; unfortunately, they recover faster than we do. As a result, he is able to grab my throat, clamping down painfully tight. Moon howls as she twists, trying to break his hold on us. Our panic escalates, knowing we face our imminent death, which has us fighting harder than either of us ever thought possible.

Slashing our claws out wildly, we hit our mark, tearing his snout open and almost removing his eye from this side of his face. As payback, he latches onto Moon's shoulder, ripping through muscle and tendons as he viciously shakes his head to increase the damage he is inflicting.

Rolling, we yank our shoulder out of his mouth, but he lunges, landing another excruciating bite to our haunches.

Raising up on our back feet, we meet his next attack with one of our own. I am aware of the massive damage done to our shoulder, as evident from the blood free-flowing down our back and leg. I cannot let this distract me because the only outcome will be our death if I do.

The unfortunate realization of this struggle is: One, he is stronger than us. Two, he has obviously been in more brawls than I have. And three, he fully intends to kill me. I don't have a hope in hell of winning since exhaustion from the fight and blood loss are quickly overtaking me. With one final swat of his paw, I slump to the ground. My desperate howls of pain do not seem to faze him as he goes in for the kill.

The pain is unlike anything we have ever experienced. I briefly contemplate shifting to end this torture faster. As the world begins to fade from around me, he releases his hold on my throat. A low growl emanates from deep in his chest. The last thing I see is him racing away from me just as I hear something moving towards me before the darkness completely overtakes us.

*****

Foster

"Foss, you know he will never agree to fight you."

"He won't have a choice because I plan to issue the challenge at the next pack meeting when every wolf is present. If he refuses, the pack will turn on him, leaving him no options other than accepting."

"Man, I think you are giving the asshole far more credit than—"

Distantly I hear the howl from a wolf, and they sound like they are in pain, making me cut Finch off, "Shhh."

"Don't shush me. You need to hear—"

"Finch, I'm serious. Did you hear that?"

"Hear what."

"A wolf howling." Finch and I walk out on the porch, and this time there is no mistaking the cries of pain. We both shift, racing toward where we believe the sounds are coming from. Mind linking with Finch, I tell him to head right while I branch to the left.

There is no doubt a fight is occurring somewhere, but as we move further into the woods, everything goes quiet. Skidding to a stop, I intently listen as I wait for the fight to start again. When it never resumes, I link back with Finch.

"Anything?"

"Not yet. I haven't heard anything for a couple of minutes, maybe…. Hang on, I see something."

"What?"

"A wolf I don't recognize."

"Where are you, Finch? Don't approach until I get there since we don't know what we are dealing with."

"I don't think the wolf is any danger to me."

"Why?"

"She's not moving."

"Where are you?" I ask as desperation creeps into my voice.

"Shit, that's a lot of blood. Thank Goddess."

"What?"

"She is definitely not one of our pack members."

"Where are you, Finch?" I yell as fear seizes my heart, and Shadow whines.

It might not be her. I don't know if I am trying to reassure him or myself.

"In the field. Oh fuck, Foss, I think she's dead."

With my heart pounding wildly in my chest, Shadow picks up his pace as we race toward where Finch is. I might have reconsidered my next question if I had known his response, "What color is she?"

"It's hard to tell because of all the blood—"

"Finch, what fucking color is her fur?"

"White." This one word causes my entire world to crash around us.

Episode Thirty-Eight: Discovery

Foster

THE SECOND I enter the field, my every nightmare is realized when I immediately recognize the injured wolf as Shay. Forcing Shadow to shift, I drop to my knees so I can begin inspecting her injuries.

Fuck, there is so goddamn much blood. Please let her be alive. I silently repeat this like a mantra to the moon Goddess, praying she will hear it and grant my request.

The second I realize she is alive, I scoop her up in my arms as I rush towards the cottage.

"Foster, who the hell is this?"

My chest tightens, and the words refuse to form, knowing how bad she is. If I can get her home, I may have a chance to save her. When I do, whoever did this to her better pray they can hide because they will face my wrath.

"Foss?"

I know I owe him an answer. After all, I may not have found her in time without him. Forcing me to finally answer him, "Shay. It's Shay."

Finch's questioning face continually glances in my direction, but thankfully he refrains from asking any of them as we race back to the cottage. Since he understood how dire her condition was, he ran ahead to get us help. Ness is a salutary who functions as a healer for our pack, barring any severe damage. In most cases, she can help an injured wolf until they are well enough to heal themselves. Shay is going to need all the help she can get if she has any chance of making it through this.

I know she is losing the battle when she involuntarily shifts back into her human form. I am almost home when I see Finch running back towards us with a blanket to cover her. Laying her down on my bed, I immediately begin inspecting the damage. I may not be a salutary, but I have had to patch myself up on more than one occasion. The worst damage is to her right shoulder, left hip, and throat.

Kill whoever did this, Shadow growls. I can't say I disagree with him. Seeing any shifter left like this would piss me off; however, this is not just any shifter; it's my mate Shay. And I am damn near on the verge of losing all control from the rage whipping through me. Shadow seems to understand regardless of how much I want to be tracking the asshole who did this to her, she needs us more.

I promise we will do that the second we know she is okay. I declare forcefully.

I no sooner have the wound on her neck cleaned up when Ness comes rushing into the room.

"What happened to her?" Ness cries as she drops her bag on the bed.

"I don't know, Nessie," I know calling her this any other time would have had her yelling at me, but now I think she is too focused on helping Shay to realize I just called her the lake serpent who lives over in Scotland.

"Let me get in here." When I don't step aside for her, she snaps, "Foster, move."

As reluctant as I am to leave her, I know she couldn't be in better hands. Ness is an adept healer; if I am being honest, Shay needs her more than she needs me hovering right now. Backing away with my hands clasped behind my head, Ness takes pity on me when she tells me, "I've got her Foss. You need to take a shower, put on some damn clothes, then have a drink while I take care of Shay."

Ness doesn't wait for my response, opting to give her full attention to the woman who probably shouldn't be alive. As I turn to leave, Ness stops me in my tracks by saying, "And when I'm done in here, we are going to have a very long and apparently overdue conversation, Foster."

Watching the crimson water swirl down the drain, knowing this is all from Shay, leaves my wolf and me itching to get out there to find out who did this to her. Technically, I could go now since Ness is here with her, but it may not be the best idea to leave them alone since we do not know who is responsible for this.

Taking Ness's advice, I grab the bottle from my cupboard and pour myself a drink. The heat from the alcohol surprisingly helps with the fury I feel. I desperately want to hunt down the asshole who hurt her and make him experience every ounce of pain he bestowed upon her. Slamming the glass down, I stalk outside just as Finch comes back through the tree line.

"Foster, is she going to be...." He trails off. I can't tell if he is more worried about her or my reaction to finding her as we did.

"I don't know," I reply as I storm by him. Finch grabs my arm, halting my progress.

"Where are you going, Foss?"

"To find the asshole who did that to her."

"Not that I disagree, but you wanna tell me why you care so much?" My teeth grind together. I know if I tell people, everything will change not only for me but for her too. Do I have the right to make this decision for both of us? I know the challenge I am getting ready to issue is dangerous; could it negatively impact Shay? If they find out she is my mate, could they use her against me? I would like to think no, but let's face it, Max is a wild card, and to be honest, I wouldn't put anything past this fucking asshole.

Without responding to his question, I push past him. I set my mind on one thing... keeping my mate safe. Especially since I have no damn idea who did this shit tonight.

"Foster, how do you know Shay?" Finch is the one person I have always told everything to. He's more of a brother to me than a cousin, and I know if I told him, he would never say anything. Besides, having an extra set of eyes watching over her wouldn't necessarily be bad. Turning to face him, he ends my emotional turmoil when he asks,

"She's your mate, isn't she?" I can't seem to confirm or deny his suspicions.

"Foster, that's how you knew who it was out there. Shay is your mate, and because of what happened to your mom, you've never wanted a mate." I drop my eyes, clearing my throat.

"The problem is she is making you rethink the whole not wanting a mate thing. Isn't she?"

"Hold the damn phone, Foster Brannon! Shay is your mate." Ness yells from her spot on the porch.

Well, if I was hoping to keep this quiet, that just flew right out the fucking window. I certainly hope Shay is ready for the onslaught from Ness. Shit, I can only hope she'll talk to me again after she finds out the one person in all of Lake who can't keep a damn secret just found out the granddaddy of them all. Yeah, I give it two hours before the entire pack knows.

Episode Thirty-Nine: Truth

Shay

TRYING TO SHAKE off the grogginess clouding my thoughts, I force my eyes open only to discover I am in a room I have never been in before. Attempting to gain my bearings, I scan my eyes around the space, and with each passing second, I have to acknowledge the simple fact I don't recognize anything. It's not until I try to move that the dull ache in my shoulder brings the memory of being attacked, slamming front and center into my thoughts.

Flinging the covers off, I leap from the bed, my heart pounding wildly. I have no fucking clue where I am, which terrifies me more than I can ever express. When I hear the doorknob twisting, I look around desperately for something to use as a weapon. I will not allow the asshole who attacked me in the woods to get the upper hand on me again.

Realizing there isn't anything in here to use, I rush forward, slamming into the door the second they try to open it. If the sound of the thud from the other side is anything to go by, I would have to say whoever it was is on their ass right now; perhaps now is my best chance at escaping. As I prepare to rip the door open, I hear a soft moan followed by,

"Damn, Shay, it's me."

"Ness?"

"Yeah. Owwww." Yanking the door open, I find her rubbing her forehead and, as suspected, lying on the floor.

"Oh my goddess, Ness. I'm so sorry. I woke up and didn't know where I was, and—" my words are coming out in a rush. She holds her hand up, waving off what I hope is the apology, not me.

"It's alright. I probably would have reacted the same way if I were in your shoes." Reaching my hand out, I help her to her feet, still muttering my regrets for knocking her on her ass.

"Are you okay?"

"Well, I can't say having a door slammed against my head has been the highlight of my day, but otherwise, I'm fine. How about you? How are you feeling?"

For the first time since I rushed the door, the thought of the attack comes slamming back in on me. My hand instinctually reaches towards my neck, followed by my shoulder.

"You're healing quite nicely. I imagine your wolf helped with that."

"So you know what I am now?"

"A shifter, yeah. It was kind of obvious when you kept shifting from your human form to your wolf while you were recovering."

"Are you going to report me to your pack's Alpha?"

"Why in the hell would I do that?"

"Because I'm rogue and on your pack's land."

Looking around, I realize once again I have no idea where I am exactly, making me ask, "We are on pack land, right?"

"We are. We're at Foster's place. They are the ones who found you." I assume the '*they*' she is referring to would be Foster and Finch. My stomach clenches into a tight knot. Not only did I invade their lands, but I also ran straight to the one person who told me in no uncertain terms he did not want to get involved with my shit. Oh god, I am in so much trouble right now.

"How does your pack deal with rogues?" I wish I could sound slightly more confident, but I'm scared shitless. I know how packs deal with wolves like me, which is not pretty. Tobias would make the rogue fight every pack member in the fighting circle simultaneously. While his brother Sebastian would cage the wolf, forcing the poor creature to face a slow, painful death as a warning to any other rogue who thought to encroach on his lands. If I had to choose one, it would be the former.

"Not really sure what you're asking me, Shay."

"My pack they made…. Forced the rogue…." Goddess, I could use a little help here. At least let me go out like a fighter, not some babbling damn idiot.

"You think for one second Foster would let anyone hurt you?"

"Why wouldn't he?" I asked, figuring she has no idea he's my mate. He has made it abundantly clear he is not interested in a mate, nor is he looking for a relationship. Oh shit, was I talking in my sleep? He is going to be so pissed at me.

She shakes her head at me as a grin covers her face. She pulls me towards the stairs, taking my hand in hers. "Come on, Shay."

Trepidation continues to mount as we descend toward the man I will have to answer to soon. Finch jumps to his feet when he sees Ness leading me downstairs. He doesn't hesitate as he rushes over to pull me in for a hug.

"Damn, you're a sight for sore eyes. Welcome back to the land of the living."

"It's good to…. be back?" my questioning tone has him pulling back some to look at me.

"Hell yeah, seeing you up and moving around is good. It was touch and go there for a couple of days."

"A coup—couple days?" I ask in a stammer.

"Shay, the attack was four days ago."

"Shit Seamus…. My job."

"Don't worry, Shay, we have kept Seamus apprised of what's happening. Hell, if we don't call him, he calls us twice a day to check up on you."

"Everything? He knows everything?"

"Of course he does. Wait, you didn't know he knew about us, did you?"

What I want to say to him is, are you dumb? In what world do we tell non-shifters about us shifters? Hell, this was a bigger no-no than being rogue in my old pack. Instead, I keep it simple, mumbling, "No."

The screen door flies open, causing my heart to drop to my feet when Foster comes storming through it with Ness hot on his heels. Heck, I didn't even realize she had gone outside. I wish I had paid attention; perhaps I would have better prepared myself for the confrontation I know will be transpiring soon.

We stand there looking at one another for what feels like an eternity, but, in reality, it is mere seconds before he shocks the ever-loving shit out of me when he storms forward and pulls me into his embrace.

*****

Brady

Natashia did precisely what I figured she would do and denied everything. She even went so far as to say Shay probably returned it to her room before she stole the money and took off. Because that makes any fucking sense at all. Yeah, she's going to steal a million dollars and run from the pack, but before she does, she returns a valuable necklace. More unbelievable is that she gave it back to the one person who treated her worse than most of the other wolves in this pack. Yeah, totally fucking believable. Okay, so apparently, Natashia is going to be zero help here, yet on the flip side, Travis is a little too fucking eager to be involved.

This leaves me with one option, Maggie.

"Maggie, I am aware you know more than you are alluding to. I promise you, I don't want to hurt Shay. To be honest, I don't think she did any of the things we accused her of."

"Why do you think I know where she is?"

"Because I know she left from the bus station. I also know the approximate time, which just so happens to correlate with the time you called to tell me you were at the station and Shay wasn't there." Maggie swallows hard. I know I only need to push a bit harder.

"Maggie, if I can find Shay, I can prove she's innocent. Don't you think we owe her this much at the very least?" At this point,

71

it's no longer just about finding Shay to prove her innocence; it is also about protecting Maggie because the more I dig into this, the more Travis questions me. Last night he informed me I just needed to give him fifteen minutes alone with her and a willingness to turn my back, and he would have Maggie giving away all her secrets. Even the ones we don't need.

Travis's activities over the last forty-eight hours further confirm he is not the man I want as my Beta. I can't say anything currently, though, not right now. My dad is pushing him to take over the role. I need to wait until I am formally made Alpha. Then I plan on changing all the things I hate about this fucking pack. Starting with ensuring bullies like Travis and my dad no longer have the pull they do now.

All steps I plan to take when I have the title. For the time being, I need to think like an Alpha but protect like a Beta. To do this, I need Maggie to believe me.

"What can I say to prove you can trust me?"

"You promise you will not kill her?" the desperation leaking into her plea is enough to make me get up and walk around to take her hand in mine.

"I promise you, Maggie. I will do everything in my power to protect her."

"She left on a bus heading towards Colorado."

Episode Forty: Punishment

Foster

I CAN'T HELP rushing over to pull her into my arms. Until last night I wasn't sure if she would make it. Let me tell you, those were the worst three days of my life. I admitted everything to Ness and Finch, confessing we knew we were each other's mates since right after she arrived in town.

Ness hit me... actually, more than once. Yelling at me until her face was beetroot red that I should have claimed her right away. I can't say I disagree after seeing what happened to her. There is a good chance I could have protected her.

"Who did this to you?" Finch asks.

Shay removing herself from my embrace has me and my wolf missing the feel of her in our arms.

"I don't know. The only wolf I've actually seen is...." Her eyes come up to mine briefly before she quietly finishes, "Is Foster's."

"Can you describe it?"

"Do you think I could have something to drink?" Ness rushes to the refrigerator, pulling out a bottle of water and some leftovers to heat up for her. Shay tells us as many details as she can remember while picking at the food.

I can tell she is uncomfortable being here; I can't imagine why. It could have something to do with the fact that I have been a complete asshole to her since we met. Then the day I deem to acknowledge her existence, I turn around and fuck it all up the second we get around other people.

You're an asshole, dickhead. Shadow's growl rumbles through my head.

Don't hold back.

Alright then, you're the lousiest fucking asshole that has ever lived.

Having heard enough of him for the time being, I push him down as I grumble, *Take a nap, furball.*

Shay's description of the events does not provide us with any clues about who attacked her. But with absolute certainty, I can say it was not a member of this pack. Because Finch and I are both essentially Delta, we train with the remaining members no less than three days a week.

The day after Shay's attack, I invited Ian, Atlas, and Denver over to explain what happened. Yes, Atlas and Denver, like Seamus, know all about the pack of shifters living outside of town, yet I have no concerns about them telling anyone because they have secrets of their own.

Atlas and Denver will use their connection with the seedier members of Lake as well as the surrounding communities to dig around. On the other hand, Ian was tasked with protection duty when Finch or I couldn't be here with Ness and Shay.

When I see Shay shifting uncomfortably in the chair, I tell everyone, "Listen, I don't think we are going to figure this out tonight, and Shay needs to rest; we can pick this up tomorrow."

When Ness and Finch each head into the room they have been sleeping in, it gives Shay and me a minute alone. "Well, I suppose I better get going. It'll take me an hour to get home, maybe longer since I don't want to—"

"First, you're not going anywhere. Second, I know I can be an asshole, but you really think I would make you walk home after everything you and your wolf—"

"Moon."

"Moon?"

"Yeah, my wolf's name. We chose Moon. It's stupid, isn't it?"

"No, quite the opposite. It's perfect. Beautiful, in fact, just like Moon is." Just like you are. What the fuck? I need to stop thinking like this. I still am not sold on the whole mate thing. I know I shouldn't hold something she had nothing to do with against her. After all, it wasn't Shay who broke my mom's heart; I still can't help how I feel.

Goddess knows this beautiful, kind girl in front of me deserves more than what I can give her. I've seen how claiming your mate can change you. It makes you dependent on their every happiness. I don't think I have it in me to do this for anyone, including her.

Shay is sitting there like she is waiting for me when I realize I didn't finish what I started to tell her. Clearing my throat, I continue, "I'm not that big of an asshole to let you and Moon walk home."

"But Seamus—"

"Said you are not to return until Tuesday at the earliest and only if you are ready."

"I wouldn't feel right imposing—"

"Well, you don't have to worry about it because you are not an imposition, Shay." She gnaws on her lower lip as her eyes move over to the door. I get a distinct feeling she is used to doing things on her own, but I also sense her hesitation. She must realize if she was to go home and whoever did this to her showed up, she is not fully healed yet, which leaves her vulnerable. I don't think she enjoys feeling this way. The problem is I can't tell if she hates depending on others or feeling vulnerable more.

"At the very least, stay another night or two, Shay. That way you can heal."

Her eyes move around the space before they settle on the couch. "I guess as long as you're sure it's no bother, I can crash on the couch."

"It's no bother, and you'll sleep in the same bed you've been sleeping in the last couple of days. Now, let's get something clean to sleep in." She reluctantly follows me back upstairs. After I give her another shirt to wear, I excuse myself to give her a few minutes to change. Apparently, I didn't give her enough time, though, because when I walked back in, she was trying to change the bandage covering her shoulder.

Yet it's not the fresh injury that draws my attention. No, what has my undivided attention is the old scars from long ago covering Shay's back that catch me off guard. She immediately snatches the shirt I left for her, hoping to hide the damage, but I storm over to stop her.

"Who did this to you, Shay?"

"It doesn't matter."

"The fuck it doesn't. Who the hell did this?"

"Foster—"

76

"Shay, tell me who did this to you."

She closes her eyes before whispering, "The Alpha and Luna from my old pack."

"They fucking…. They…. Why would they do this to you?" I ask as I run my hand over her back. She instantly pulls away from the contact.

"As punishment."

"Punishment for what? What the fuck could you have possibly done to deserve…." Anger rips through me, choking the words in my throat.

"Because of my dad…. My family was…." she averts her eyes before she brings her hands up to cover her face. The sound of her sucking in a deep breath infuriates me even more. Without thinking, I reach over to pull her into my arms. Smoothing her hair, she buries her face against my shoulder. There is no goddamn way she deserved what they did to her.

For her to have sustained the kind of damage to cause this, they would have had to have beaten her and then prevented her from shifting. Otherwise, her wolf would have healed her faster than the scars could have formed.

Without thinking, I kiss the top of her head before I ask the most important question I need her to answer. "What was the name of your previous pack?"

Episode Forty-One: Details

Shay

LAST NIGHT WHEN Foster saw the scars and began questioning me, I felt like all the air in the room was sucked out. My mind started racing as my emotions overwhelmed me. Fear they would turn their back on me once they discovered the truth. Shame knowing I would have to reveal my family's background as traitors. Anger that the past I ran from has found its way back to my present, but mostly humiliation because of all the people to see my disgrace... it had to be him.

But instead of him turning his back on me in disgust, he held me until the world no longer felt like it was spinning around me. I know I can no longer hide my past from them since they are all patiently waiting for me to tell them my story.

"They branded my dad a traitor, my mom the wife of a traitor."

"What did your dad do?" Ness asks gently.

"He refused to kill a female pack member."

"Why would your Alpha want one of their pack members killed?"

"She was interfering with his plans. The direction he wanted to take the pack in, so he ordered my dad to kill her, but he couldn't do it. When Tobias found out that not only did he let her go, but he helped her escape pack lands, he was furious. The only option my dad had was to challenge him for Alpha."

"I take it your dad didn't win?" Finch asks softly.

"No. No, my dad didn't win. In truth, I think he knew he didn't stand a chance against Tobias, but he thought they would grant mom and me clemency within the pack. After all, his decisions alone put him in the fighting circle that day."

"Why didn't he just take you and leave?" Ness's question is something I've asked myself a thousand times. Life as a rogue is, without a doubt, better than death.

"He was afraid of what would happen to us, even though my mom begged him to go. When he issued the challenge, he was banking on the pack taking care of us if he fell."

"So what happened?" I notice Ness and Finch are the only ones asking me any questions. Foster is sitting stone-faced with his hands clenched together. In fact, I think the only movement coming from him is the occasional tick I see on his jawline.

"Dad lost, and he killed my mom immediately after for being the wife of a traitor. She was still holding my hand when he slashed her neck open. As for me, Tobias wanted to kill me too, but his chosen Luna Adela stepped in to stop him."

"At least she had some sense." I give Finch a slight smile he believes is my agreement. I don't have the heart to tell him the truth, but I don't have to say anything because Foster does it for me.

"She didn't do it out of the kindness of her heart. She did it to torture Shay." Foss may have spoken, but he still refuses to look up from his white-knuckled hands. Finch and Ness, however, both whip their heads in my direction.

"She saw a maid, a cook, a built-in pup sitter—"

"And a whipping post," Foster mutters through gritted teeth.

"That's not true, is it?" Ness's gaze moves from me to Foster. For the first time since I sat down, his eyes met mine as he waited for me to tell them the truth. "Tell me it's not true, Shay."

For the first time in my life, I feel completely stripped bare. I have nothing to protect me from the brutal truth of what they are asking me, "When I didn't listen...." I drop my eyes for only the third time in my adult life I feel tears filling them. "When I disappointed them or disobeyed...."

"They beat her." Foster finishes for me, and honestly, I don't know if it's worse hearing him say it, having to be the one to admit it, or living with the knowledge they all know.

"Disappointed them? What the hell could you have possibly done to disappoint them enough for them to hit you?"

"It didn't take much."

"She wasn't permitted to run with her wolf; the fuckers didn't even grant her wolf a name." this time, when I look at him, I discover the shining eyes of a wolf fighting to break free. The rigid cords in his neck, his bared teeth, and his furrowed brow reveal the rage currently coursing through him.

"Oh Goddess, Shay, they shouldn't have made you live like that."

"It's okay, Ness." The first of her tears spill over her eyelashes and tumbles down her face.

80

"No, please don't cry. I didn't mean to make you cry." I feel like an ass seeing her cry. Ness has such a soft, caring heart I should have never told her about my life, more so when Finch stands up and pulls me into his embrace, whispering softly.

"No one should have to live like that, Shay. What they did to you…. It wasn't right, and they don't deserve to have someone like you." His eyes come up to mine before he finishes. "Anyone who doesn't see how amazing you are doesn't fucking deserve you."

*****

Foster

Ouch, nothing like going in for the kill shot, but he's right. I don't deserve Shay. I wish she wasn't my mate so she could find someone who is capable of giving her the happiness she deserves. This strong woman has gone through so fucking much throughout her short life. Many others would have crumbled under the life she was forced to live. Which is a testament to her character. I know there's more to her story; I simply don't know if I can listen to any more of it tonight without completely losing my shit.

Storming outside, I waste no time shifting. Running with my wolf always clears my head. I can only hope tonight is not different. I end up in the same spot I found her all those nights ago. The memory of her laying there unresponsive, covered in blood, brings the same feelings of rage, concern, and helplessness I felt that night.

I know it's a long shot after all this time, but if I still want to catch the bastard who did this to her. I need to start somewhere. The area we found her in is my best chance of locating any evidence regarding who may have done this. Especially since Shay does not know who it was, and neither Finch nor I saw anything. After spending about an hour out here, Finch arrives.

"Why the hell would you leave Shay and Ness alone?" I can't believe he would do something so reckless. If they get hurt....

"I didn't."

"Who's with them then?" Even through our mind link, he can sense the frustration in my tone.

"Shay insisted on going home, Foss." Shadow's growls have Finch's wolf, Rom, cowering submissively.

"What was I supposed to do, Foster? Tie her up and lock her in your room?"

Yes. Shadow barks.

No. I quickly counter. "No, you did the right thing. Shay's been caged enough throughout her life. I'll call Atlas and ask him to have his guys keep an eye on her. Did Ness take her home?"

"Yes. So, what are you doing out here?"

"Hunting."

"Hunting?"

"Yeah, I'm hunting the asshole who did this, and when I find him, he will regret ever harming Moon or Shay."

Finch does not hesitate; he immediately begins searching the area. As we fan out, I pick up the scent of a wolf I don't recognize. The second I bolt in the direction I believe the wolf to be in, Finch is right behind me. Rounding the corner, I only caught a glimpse of the brownish-red fur of a male wolf about a hundred yards ahead of us before he disappeared into the thickest part of the brush.

Picking up our pace, we try to catch the intruder. The instant I see the size and color of his fur, I realize it matches the description Shay provided of the wolf who attacked her. Because one thing I know for sure is that this is most definitely not a wolf from our pack.

As we chase him, I wonder if this wolf could be someone from Shay's old pack. Based on what I have learned about them so far, I would not put anything past them. I can't imagine they were too happy when they lost her.

The wolf is fast, but I'm quicker, and stride-for-stride, Shadow and I are catching up with this fucker. He shifts directions, bolting into some thicker brush, and I momentarily lose sight of him. Pushing myself harder, I burst out of the tree line just in time to see the taillights from the truck speeding away.

"Fuck!" Shifting back, I bend over, trying to catch my breath as Finch arrives at my side.

"Did you see who it was?"

"No, but now I know what the asshole's wolf looks like, and more importantly, I have his scent."

Episode Forty-Two: Oh Hell No

Shay

TODAY IS THE first day since Ness dropped me off that I am leaving the house. I have a shift at Stooges tonight, and even though Seamus stopped by yesterday to check on my progress and tell me I don't have to come in if I'm still not at a hundred percent, I feel like I am taking advantage of his generosity. So hi-ho hi-ho, it's off to work I go. Honestly, it feels good to get out of the house and do something productive.

Two hours into my shift and Mandy still has not spoken to me. Jerry has toasted my return seven times, and Hyde has hugged me five times. I guess Seamus just told everyone I was involved in an accident. Hyde took that to mean a car accident.

"Welcome back, Shay." Looking up, I discover one of the guys I met the night of the dart tournament. He's one of the guys who works at the mill and was extremely nice to me that entire night. He has stopped in a couple times since then, normally having a drink or two before telling me how nice it was to see me again and leaving me a large tip.

"Hi."

"Sean."

"Hello, Sean. Can I get you something?" I ask him with a smile.

"I'll take whatever you have on tap." '

Since the bar is not that busy, Mandy volunteers to leave early; however, her idea of knocking off early for the day doesn't actually involve leaving. Nope. Instead, she walks to the other side of the bar, plops her ass down on the stool next to Sean, and immediately begins flirting.

Her touchy-feely advances seem to make Sean uncomfortable. I'm not sure why she keeps looking over at me.

Normally, Mandy refuses to acknowledge my existence... well, unless her ass is parked on the other side of the bar. Even then, it only happens when barking at me to get her a drink. And it seems tonight is no exception. This crazy girl goes so far as to wave me off dismissively when I tell her how much she owes.

Just when I think she has forgotten about her love affair with Foster, he comes in, and she drops her shiny new toy, like yesterday's news. This must make him happy since Sean seems to breathe a sigh of relief.

I suppose it's Foster's turn, and the more I think about it, the more I know they are perfect for one another. He's a jerk who gives me whiplash from his abrupt shifting split personalities since he's back to ignoring me, and she's a bitch whose hateful scowls could rival any good serial killer.

I guess the whole flirt with Sean thing was Mandy's way of getting back at me. Getting back at me for what I can't say. Does she think I'm interested in him, or he's into me? It wouldn't surprise me, but I gotta say I don't have the foggiest idea where she came up with this shit.

I get an onslaught of people needing drinks all at once, and I rush around trying to fill the orders. You would think Mandy would bring her ass back over here to help me but nope. It seems she's busy draping her arms around Foster as she chats with him and Finn.

When the last beer is served, I take a deep breath and blow a piece of unruly hair from my face while I check stock in the coolers.

"So I was wondering if I could take you out for a cup of coffee?" Okay, so talk about left field. Maybe Mandy knows more than I give her credit for. I wonder if he has been in here asking about me, and that's how she knew. I don't miss Foster glaring in our direction like he's waiting for my answer too.

"That's really nice, but I think I'll have to take a pass." Sean's smile drops as disappointment settles across his features. I feel bad seeing him like this. Feeling like I owe him an explanation, I elaborate, "I don't get off until midnight."

"I don't mind waiting, and the café is open all night." I guess it couldn't hurt; it's just coffee.

"Okay."

"Yeah?"

"Sure." I don't miss the low growl coming from Foster's direction.

When my shift ends, I find Sean waiting patiently for me by the door. We no sooner start towards his car when the door slams open behind me.

Spinning, I find Foster standing there, jaw set, eyes ablaze as he levels his focus on Sean. Sean wisely takes a step away as the extremely pissed-off shifter stalks toward him.

Stepping between them, I ask, "Is everything okay?"

"No, everything is not fucking okay. Do I look okay to you, Shay?" Foster snarls.

"We're just going to get a cup—"

"I'm well aware," Foster cuts me off; however, when Sean steps toward me to take my arm in his hand, a low menacing growl rumbles deep in Foster's chest. "I advise you not to put your fucking hands on her."

His eyes are glowing brighter than firelight, and I know Shadow will force the shift if Sean stays here. Nothing will stop Shadow from attacking if he puts his hands on me.

"Shay?" Sean's questioning tone does nothing to hide the fear he feels facing Foster.

"I suggest you leave now."

"It's okay, Sean. I'll see you later," I tell him, hoping to defuse whatever the hell is going on right now.

"Not fucking likely." Foster snaps. When Sean doesn't listen to his warning, Foster takes a step closer to him.

Sean slowly begins backing away from us when he has a wide enough berth between Foss and him; he asks, "Will you be okay, Shay?"

Foster begins moving towards him again, issuing his final warning, "GET. THE. FUCK. OUT. OF. HERE!"

I snatch his arm to stop him before he can charge forward and hurt this poor guy whose only offense is asking me to have a cup of coffee. Coffee. Christ, this is quickly becoming a shit show.

When Sean is safely in his car, speeding out of the parking lot, I look at Foster. His eyes are still shining bright, but I imagine mine are right now too.

"What the hell was that all about?"

"Why did you agree to go out with that…. That asshole?"

"First off, he is a nice guy. Second, the only asshole around here currently is you. And third, I don't owe you a goddamn explanation. However, you owe me a huge one."

One word is uttered, and I can tell right away it's not Foster saying it; it's Shadow, "Mate."

"Oh hell no, you don't get to use our forced bond as a reason for how you acted. I refuse to let you use this against me. Especially since you made it abundantly fucking clear that you don't want a mate, so you don't get to pull this shit when another man shows interest in me."

"Shay—"

"I said no, Foster. Listen, you have two options here: either cut the mate bond or man the fuck up." I have no damn idea why I added the second part. What the hell is wrong with me? Not waiting for his response, I turn to storm away.

The entire way home, and even once I'm locked safely in my house, I continually mutter through clenched teeth, "As if I need another asshole thinking he can fucking go all caveman when someone likes me but ignore me any other time."

Yanking the sweater off, I toss it into the dirty clothes before I pull my hair up in a messy bun to begin my nighttime routine. When someone knocks on my door, I am not afraid for the first time ever. Since I currently have enough adrenaline rushing through my veins, I could probably take on King motherfucking Kong. Thankfully, the oversized ape is not what I find when I jerk open the door. Nope, just a jackass.

"What the hell are you doing here, Foster?"

"Manning up," He responds before he backs me against the wall with his lips smashed against mine.

The kiss is primal, wild, all-consuming, and everything I have ever fantasized it would be since the first time I saw him. His hands are on my hips, his body pressed against mine. The hard lines of his frame compete with the solid wall behind me.

This time, the growl coming from him is no longer menacing; it's deep and filled with wanton need. I have never wanted to be claimed. Never... not once... until now.

Right here—right now, with his hands sliding over my body, his lips erasing every thought other than the magnificent man before me. I know I would submit to our bond without a second thought.

"Shay," my name whispered from the lips still pressed against mine, has heat racing through me, settling deep in my core. The tingling sensation he is causing overwhelms my every thought. His hand glides along my side. His thumb brushes over my breast, causing my body to immediately respond to his touch as my nipple hardens.

My mind flashes with images of him taking me against the wall, his tongue teasing the nipple he just woke up.

His hand travels down my side, slipping around my hips and under my ass so he can lift me.

My legs seem to have taken on a mind of their own as they instinctually wrap around his waist. I can't deny the jolt of desire flooding through me when I feel the hard length of his arousal rubbing against my soaking-wet folds.

When I move my hips to be closer, the exquisite friction it produces has a low moan racing up my throat.

Pawing at his shirt, I am desperate to feel his skin against mine. As my fingertips graze over his skin as I drag it up, his bare flesh responds and prickles in their wake.

His mouth moves from my lips to my neck as he nips and sucks at my overly sensitive skin. Every touch, every kiss, every flick of his tongue sends an electric pulse from the point of contact straight between my legs to the place I am desperate to have him touch.

When I think I cannot take any more, he increases the dampness between my legs when he carries me into my room.

Episode Forty-Three: Claiming

Shay

$\mathcal{B}$Y THE TIME he kicks the door open to my bedroom, I have his shirt off, and I am nimbly working on the button to his jeans.

He stops just short of the bedside, and as reluctant as I am to do this, my legs uncoil from around his waist. He pulls back just enough to pull my tank top over my head. His eyes are shining as bright as the sun.

Two golden orbs burn intensely from his unbridled desire.

Desire I make him feel. His yearning to be near me, touch me, please me... is only rivaled by my need to experience everything he wants to give.

Our ragged panting breath from the kiss increases the heat coiling low in my belly. I have never craved the touch of someone as much as I yearn for Foster's.

"Shay, if you want me to stop, you will have to tell me because I am incapable of doing it on my own."

Shaking my head, the hint of a smile tips his lips, but he refuses to let me get away with this, "Use your words here, Shay. I want to hear you say it. Tell me what you want from those perfectly delicious lips of yours."

"You. I want you. I don't want you to stop." He reaches up, pulling the band out of my hair, allowing my blonde locks to tumble down around my shoulders.

"You are the most beautiful woman I have ever seen. Utterly fucking exquisite."

My hands begin slowly lowering my pants. Teasing him, giving him small glimpses of skin one gradual slip at a time.

When I step out of my jeans and look back up, his pupils are blown wide as he draws in a generous gulp of air. Seeing him looking at me like he is the hunter and I am the prey has the hair on my arm rising as goosebumps cover my skin.

The absolute rush I feel holding this amount of power over him is intoxicating. Reaching up, he wraps his fist in my hair, bringing it to his nose to inhale it deeply.

"I want to hear you moan my name."

A shiver passes through me, thinking about all the things he can do to make this desire of his a reality. Biting my lip, I try to imagine those lips on me, tasting me, taking me to the edge: one lick, one suck, one nibble at a time. I want that; I want it more than I want oxygen right now.

Without warning, my thought spills out for him to hear as I ask with a breathy whisper, "Promise?"

He gives me that promise just before he smashes his lips against mine. "Over and over and over again. Until you don't have the strength to say anything else."

Running his tongue over my lips, I submit to him as I greedily invite his chasing tongue into my mouth. He tastes like the

92

nutty, oaky mix from the bourbon he drank at the bar and a sweetness that is all Foster.

His nimble fingers make short work snapping open the clasp holding my bra in place. As the thumb on his left hand circles my nipple, the other slides below the lace, covering my throbbing center slick from the anticipation of his touch.

My stomach clenches tight when his hand finds its mark, and with the first sweep of his fingers, I come unglued, moaning into his mouth.

Arching to bring myself closer to what I truly seek, I feel the length of his erection press against me. The desperate ache for him to fill me is only partially sated when he dips one, followed by a second finger inside me.

"So fucking wet. I can't wait to feel you around me," Foster whispers against my neck.

His hand is moving, circling, dipping, exploring, and the wetness is coating the inside of my thighs.

My skin is on fire, my body buzzing from the orgasm threatening to explode, and when he sucks my nipple into his hot mouth, that is precisely what I do; I explode. The intensity has my knees buckling.

Withdrawing his fingers, another wave of desire racks my already overheated body when he brings them to his mouth to suck them clean.

"Do you have any fucking idea how delicious you taste?" My cheeks burn red hearing him say this. I have never done this before. If I tell him I'm still a virgin, will he change his mind and end the glorious feelings he is producing?

"Answer me, Shay. Do you have any idea?" He asks while inching my panties down, and I would say or do anything right now to experience everything he is offering.

Marcelle Valentine

Slowly shaking my head, he clicks his tongue, skimming his lips over mine before he demands, "Ahhh–ahhh, use your words, Shay. I want to hear you tell me if you know how delicious you are."

"N—no." Heat floods my cheeks because no matter how turned on I am. No matter how much I want him to keep doing what he's doing, telling him this is terrifying. I'm inexperienced, and the thought he may not enjoy it as much as I am makes me unsure.

"No, what?"

"No.... I–I don't know."

"Don't know what?" Why can't he let this go?

"How de-delicious I taste," my timid response as I drop my eyes has him pulling my face up to look at him.

"It's like fucking nirvana. I could live between those thighs." This time, he brings his mouth fully to mine, probing my lips with his tongue until I relent and part them for him.

Tasting myself on his tongue has the ache building all over again. He lays me back on the bed before he kisses his way down my body.

His hot breath teasing my nipples has me groaning his name.

"That's one."

He takes a nipple into his mouth while his thumb circles my clit. The way he's touching me is blissful, and I want more. I need this man to take me over and over until I am so spent I can't move. The mere thought has me lifting my hips, hoping he'll slide his fingers in my pussy so I can come again.

When he releases my nipple, I pray he will move to the other side, and when he does, his name slips out with a throaty moan.

"Two."

94

Moving lower, he sucks the skin from my lower abdomen lightly into his mouth while his free hand grazes over each breast.

"Fuck, Foster. I don't…. I can't."

"I'll accept that as three. Oh, and Shay, you can and you will."

I never thought I would be one of those women who would like a man dominating me but right now, I don't care what he does, how he does it, or the demands Foster is making of me as long as he doesn't stop I will eagerly submit to them all.

Sliding between my legs, I gasp as his tongue swipes across me. I try to sit up; however, his hand on my stomach halts any further movement.

"I know what I'm doing, beautiful. So just lay back and enjoy because I know I sure as hell plan to."

Panting, I almost hate that I am getting ready to say this, but I need to be honest, "But…."

"But what?" He follows his question with a kiss on each thigh.

"I don't."

"Don't what?"

"Know what I'm doing."

"You've never been with anyone before?" His eyes are bright as he slides his tongue over my center, giving my clit a quick kiss.

My entire body feels energized, yet the sensation that there is not enough oxygen in the world to fill my lungs overwhelms me as I shiver under him.

"Use your words, Shay." Again with the tongue. If he keeps doing this, I am going to lose my fucking mind. With another swipe across my clit, I am on the edge of the orgasm he wants me to have, and the overwhelming sensation has me falling back on the bed.

"Foster."

"That's four, but I'm still waiting for your answer."

"No. No, I've never been with another man before."

A growl rumbles from his chest. At first, I think he's pissed, but when I look up, I discover wickedly excited eyes staring back at me. Seeing him like this, positioned between my legs, lips shining from my previous orgasm, sends tingles rushing to my extremities. His eyes refuse to leave mine as he returns to lavishing his full attention on me.

The climax this time rips through me. Foster does not relent, even as I scream his name. Pulling away from me, he runs his fingers over my thighs before saying, "Five, and we don't have to—"

I don't allow him to finish his sentence as I crash my mouth on his, yanking him on top of me. I whimper when I realize he still has his pants on. Desperate to have him fill the burning ache within me, I paw at his pants.

Having reached the end of his immense control, he stands to remove them. Even though I had never had sex before, seeing him standing there completely turned on and filled with want has my desire building, knowing he will soon fill me and satisfy the burning need consuming every piece of me.

He settles between my legs, and for the first time in my life, I am vibrating with need, feeling his erection pressed against me. Lifting my hips, I grind against him, praying he will finally give me what I am on the verge of begging for.

"Shay," he moans as he slowly pushes inside me.

"Are you okay?" I nod because I can't respond. I'm better than okay I'm on the edge of paradise.

The pain from having a man inside me is there, but so is the pleasure. And the knowledge that Foster, my mate, is the one who is doing it only increases the euphoria I am experiencing.

"That's one, handsome."

He grins as he slowly slides in and out. I meet each thrust of his hips with a grind of my own. It doesn't take long before all the pain is gone, and the only thing remaining is the pleasure he provides. Pushing for him to move faster as he skillfully builds me back up, I can't help but moan his name, "Foster."

"Six. I want to feel you come, Shay."

We continue this frenzy until he rolls, pulling me on top of him. Not sure what to do, I listen to my body as his hands on my hips help guide me.

The faster I move, the higher I climb, and before long, I find myself on the edge of a cliff. I want to fall, to tumble into the erotic abyss he provides. The desire I feel for this man is something I never knew existed.

Even my attraction for Brady cannot compare to the satisfaction I have feeling him building under me, filling me up, and this time when I come, he falls with me.

"Shay." "Foster." We both scream.

Episode Forty-Four: Unworthy

Foster

βEING ABLE TO hold Shay in my arms, the taste of her still lingering on my tongue, and the honeysuckle scent of her soft hair surrounding me have me questioning my sanity for refusing to see what was right in front of me. This beautiful, magnificent, gentle soul, the moon goddess granted Shadow and me, is everything we have ever needed.

I'm not worthy of such a gift, especially after how I treated her.

The memory of her giving herself to me fully, submitting to my every demand, has my dick twitching with my need to feel her around me again.

The overwhelming desire to claim her when I was buried deep inside her became too much. Had I not rolled over to put her on top, moving that spot on her neck far from my fangs, I would have done just that. Still, before I take this step, we need to have a candid conversation because she yet has the right to refuse.

Truth be told, after the way I treated her, I wouldn't blame her if she did.

I realize, in some ways, I didn't treat her much better than her previous pack did, which causes a jumble of emotions. Fury at them for hurting her, disgust at myself for subjecting her to this, and amazement at the immense strength this woman possesses.

Running my fingers over her back, feeling the raised scars, I find myself again questioning how anyone could have done this to her. The soft sigh she gives me confirms this time she does not oppose my touch against her.

"Sorry, I didn't mean to wake you."

Stretching, she turns before curling into me. Her lips against my chest when she gives me a soft kiss causes my dick to more than twitch this time. If she keeps this up, she will soon find me settled between her silky thighs again.

"Mm mm, if you want to start or continue that count, I'm happy to have you wake me."

"I do like the way you think, beautiful."

I feel her tense against me, "What's the matter."

"I'm not beautiful. Moon, she's beautiful. I'm just scarred."

"Shay, I don't give a shit about these marks. Even if they weren't there, I couldn't find you any more attractive than I do now."

"I call bullshit," she smiles, but it lacks any genuine happiness. Taking her hand, I show her how wrong she is.

"This is what you do to me, beautiful." Her hand wraps around my dick, which is rock hard and standing at full attention.

She huffs, rolling her eyes at me while she counters, "Doesn't count."

I notice her hand is still wrapped around my shaft and she has begun slowly stroking me, making it hard to think of anything beyond fucking her. "What's that supposed to mean?"

"It means...." she leans in, kissing my neck, and briefly, I could give a shit less what it means because Shadow is now screaming for us to take her again. "from what I understand, this can happen if the wind blows right."

"This?" I ask her teasingly.

"Yeah, you know." She squeezes her hand, increasing her pace. I fully intend on coming inside her, not in her hand. If I want to do this, I need to slide into her sooner rather than later.

Rolling over, she glides the tip of my erection to her center. The warm wetness instantly begins coating my dick. I couldn't stop the growl racing through me if I wanted to as I started slowly thrusting in and out of her.

"First off, 'this,' as you so eloquently put it, is called a penis, a dick, a cock, take your pick, and what I have is an erection. Second, Shay, I can assure you I have never got an erection because the wind blew. Third, I have never wanted or responded to any other woman's touch as I do yours. Finally, everything about you turns me on. From these beautiful blue eyes to this magnificent body of yours, to the way your body forms around mine. I knew I wanted you desperately from the first time I saw you, even though I told myself I didn't, but when I tasted you just now, I knew—"

Shay cuts me off, kissing me more fervently than I have ever experienced. Grabbing her leg, I pull it up to kiss it before I devour her perfect breasts. She must enjoy what I'm doing because her hands rake up my back and tangle in my hair.

If I had enough willpower, I would bury my face between these legs lapping her up until she is screaming my name, but she feels so fucking good wrapped around my cock I don't think I could last long enough to sink my dick back into her.

The thrust of my hips met by her every upward stroke has me rocketing ever closer to the high from the climax she provides. I have to admit, hearing the sound of my body slapping against hers is a huge fucking turn on.

"Come with me, Shay."

"Yes, so close."

"So fucking tight." I need to slow down if I don't want to finish ahead of her. But when her walls clamp around me, sucking me further inside her, I know she has reached the peak. I slam once more before I spill inside her.

Okay, while I am not complaining, I would happily do this all night. I didn't mean to. I wanted to learn more about her. But if I keep kissing her breasts and licking her nipples, I will do just that. Which is why I roll off her and pull her against me.

"Tell me about your parents."

"I don't remember much I was only five when they died."

"What do you remember?"

"I remember how my mom smelled, the happy feeling I got when I heard my dad's booming laugh."

Tucking a piece of unruly hair behind Shay's ear, I take her hand in mine as I listen to her talk about parents she probably hasn't spoken of prior to coming to Lake.

"I remember how my dad would dance my mom around the kitchen singing completely off-key." This makes me laugh cause I totally relate; I couldn't sing if my life depended on it.

"I remember how my mom looked at my dad like he was the only other soul in the world." Like I am looking at you, I think to myself.

"I remember my dad reading to me each night before I went to bed and my mom kissing my head when he finished the story."

I don't know what it means to care about a father, but my mom…. She was everything to me. That is, until she curled in on herself and forgot how to live.

When my dad rejected her, he broke every piece of her heart. I never understood how anyone could have this kind of hold over another until she came waltzing into my life. I was too damn stubborn to see it, but Shay has taken every brick I placed and has removed them one at a time. Breaking apart the wall I built to protect myself from anything that could hold as much sway as my father did over my mom.

"But mostly, I remain proud of him."

"Proud?"

"Yeah, he stood up for his convictions even though he knew he would suffer for them. He chose what was right over what was easy. He will forever be the person I most look up to."

"I take it this was the choice that resulted in him having to issue the challenge to your Alpha and ultimately cost him his life in the fighting circle?"

"Yes," she quietly whispers.

"What was it he did?"

"He let someone go."

"So you told us, who was the person he let go?" I run my thumb over her hand. I want to know everything about her; this seems to be the most important issue of her life. The one that put her at the mercy of a useless fucking Alpha, by the one I plan on paying a visit to someday, very soon. I just need to wrap up my pack business.

"She was the Alpha's true mate; he rejected her because he deemed her unworthy of being his Luna." Yet another reason to despise this asshole.

"He is such a useless prick. He didn't want her to be his Luna, but it was alright to sleep with her. To make matters worse, he got her pregnant. That is when his chosen mate Adela demanded Tobias kill her, along with their unborn pup."

"You have got to be shitting me."

"I shit you not, handsome, but Tobias couldn't do it. For all of Alpha Matthews's bluster, he's a spineless asshole, so he sent my dad instead. When dad found her, he couldn't do it. As a result, dad helped her escape, and…. Well, you know the rest."

"I'm sorry, Shay. I'm sorry your pack Alpha abused his power and took your family. They didn't deserve it, and you sure as shit didn't deserve what they did to you."

"I guess it made me who I am. It brought me to Lake." The rest is spoken in the hope I would not hear her. "Brought me to you."

"I'm glad you're here."

"So am I. You know I think about her sometimes."

"Who?"

"The woman my dad saved. I think about her and wonder if she made it. If she's okay. If her son helped heal her broken heart."

"Maybe we can try to find out. Do you remember what her name is by chance?"

"Only her first name."

"We can try to figure out the rest. Tell me what it is."

"Fay? Yeah, her name was definitely Fay."

My entire world tilts hearing this as my heart beats frantically in my chest.

It can't fucking be.

There is no goddamn way she could be talking about my mom.

Episode Forty-Five: Disclosure

Brady

HAVING LEFT MY office since no one in this pack feels the need to knock before entering, I prefer to avoid just anyone walking in on us. So I went to the one place I figured no one would bother us, the kitchen.

"You're sure?"

"Yes."

"Why would she go there?"

"I don't know; I can only tell you it was Colorado."

"What about Colorado?" Travis asks when he walks in on us talking in the kitchen.

Son of a bitch! There were only four people I absolutely did not want to hear that, and he is at the top of this list. He will not hesitate to tell my dad, who is number one on the damn thing. I know I need to say something, but it is not me who answers him; it's Nan. I'm amazed at how quick she came up with this.

"It is where we purchase the Alpha's favorite lamb from."

"Lamb."

"Yes, sir." Nan turns to look at him, yet her eyes never meet his. I don't know why I never paid attention to this before. Now that I have, I can't unsee it, and it pisses me off that any member of this pack feels they are beneath anyone else. But what upsets me more is I have been a part of the problem all along.

"Yeah, I asked Nan to make dad's favorite meal the night of the Alpha ceremony."

"So why is Maggie telling Nan where to get the meat from?"

"She wasn't telling Nan; she was telling me. I don't understand why you're questioning any of this." My tone drops dangerously low. He wisely takes a step back. For several minutes, Travis remains in the kitchen as Nan fires questions about the Alpha, hoping to keep up the ruse. After he leaves and I confirm he is not lingering in the hall, Nan pulls me back into the kitchen.

"Mister Brady, you have to get to Shay first. If he finds her, he will kill her."

"Why?"

"I believe he had something to do with why she left. The way he would look at her like he owned her.... It was disturbing."

"Why didn't you ever say anything?"

Nan tilts her head, her earnest eyes beseeching me to understand without forcing her to say anything. I imagine whatever she has to say will not be easy to hear or for her to disclose.

"This pack did not treat Shay kindly. Not by anyone here. I love her like the daughter I always wanted. I was just afraid to show it. Scared of what Adela would do to me if I did. I should

106

have done more for her, but so should both of you." Her eyes move from mine to Maggie's, whose shame is apparent. We both know what she is telling us is true. We should have done better.

Nan's demeanor changes and I believe she instantly regrets saying this to me. I'm sure she thinks she is going to get in trouble. Nothing could be farther from the truth.

"I assure you, Nan, I am going to do everything in my power to protect her and bring her back to her home, where I will promise you, Shay, and every other fucking member of this pack that you will all be treated as an equal from here on out."

"Then you should move fast."

*****

Foster

I made some lame ass excuse after she told me the name of the woman her dad saved so I could leave. I need to know if they are one and the same person, and I know of only one individual who may be able to answer this for me; my aunt Claire.

I know my sudden departure left Shay questioning what happened, but if her dad saved my mom, how can I ever look her in the eyes again? In a sense, she lost her parents because of…. Because of me. The simple fact is he saved this woman by defying his Alpha because she was pregnant. I guess no one could say for sure if he would have released her if she wasn't, but he admitted he was not able to kill her when she begged for the life of her unborn pup. For a Beta, this is unheard of. Even Ian doesn't outright defy Deacon. He may encourage me

107

to look into his questionable dealings, but he would never outright refuse him, which further confirms the character of her dad. A man who was worth more than the Alpha who took his life, murdered his wife, and enslaved his daughter.

Stopping to grab some coffee and breakfast, I am waiting for her at the kitchen table. The house is still quiet; however, I know it won't be much longer before she wakes since my aunt is always up by five in the morning.

"Foss? I didn't expect to see you here this morning. Did I forget you were coming over?"

"No, you didn't forget anything Aunt Claire," I say as I stand to kiss her cheek and wait for her to take her seat. Something she taught me from an early age. Advising this is what a gentleman does. In fact, she would smack the back of my head if I didn't.

"I brought breakfast."

"Oh, that's so lovely. Let me go wake Ness and Finch."

"Actually, do you think we could talk alone for a few minutes? Then we can wake them."

"Is something wrong, son?" Even though she never pretended to be my mom, and she did everything in her power to help me remember my mom, which helped her remember her sister, at times like this, she always wanted me to know she loved me every bit as much as Finch. Thank god Finn thought of me like a brother and never took offense to this.

Swallowing, I do not know how to begin this conversation with her. How do you ask someone who refuses to acknowledge my father's existence to tell me about him?

"Foster, you know you can tell me anything," she advises as she places her hand on top of mine.

108

Taking a deep breath, I blow it out before I respond with, "Can I also ask you anything?"

"Of course, you can. Does this have anything to do with the young woman Ness has been talking about?"

"No. Yes.... I don't know, maybe."

She smiles as she tilts her head, and I know I am confusing her. Deciding the best course of action is to rip the bandaid off, I say, "What was my father's name?"

Her face instantly drops as she sits back in her chair. "Why would you want to know about that lousy son of a... you know the rest?"

"Trust me, it's not something I ever thought I would be doing."

"Then why ask?"

"I... Shay...." Why is this so damn hard to say? It is as simple as these ten words; I think Shay's dad saved mom and me from him. But as easy as they are to mutter in my head, they refuse to cross my lips.

"Foss, I can't help you if you don't talk to me."

"It's really hard, aunt Claire. I never wanted to know anything about him. I would be fine with knowing nothing about him for the rest of my days and his, but I don't think this is an option any longer."

"I don't understand."

"It's a suspicion I have. One I can't talk to anyone else about. I pray I'm wrong, but if I'm not...."

"Your sperm donor showed up out of the blue one day, uninvited and, in my opinion, completely unwanted. The second Faye saw him standing there looking all masculine, her words, not mine, there was no turning back. Your mom decided to leave the pack when that.... That pig didn't get whatever he wanted from our Alpha. I tried to talk her out of it. Some of it was because I couldn't bear the thought of losing my best friend and the only sibling I had, but it wasn't the only reason something about him rubbed me the wrong way, and I wasn't the only one who felt like this. Our Alpha also tried to convince her to wait. Alpha wanted to get to know him and his pack better. Especially since his pack was several states away. It wasn't like we could be there in an hour if she needed us, but Faye was determined. Actually, smitten would be a better word to describe it. She was utterly smitten by him, where I just found him to be a smug, pompous a-hole."

"Why was she so struck by him?"

"He was the future Alpha. But more important was something she didn't immediately disclose, and he never did; they were mates. I don't know if withholding this was her idea or his; if I had to venture a guess, I would say it was his since Faye told me everything."

"Aunt Claire, what was his name?"

"Tobias, Tobias Matthews."

"Well Fuck," I mutter.

Time to kill the useless son of a bitch. Shadow retorts.

Episode Forty-Six: Life Lessons

Shay

$\mathcal{I}$ KNOW I am not as experienced sexually as most of the other women he's been with but having someone you just had sex with twice just up and leave while giving some stupid-ass excuse can't be a good sign.

Goddess, why did I practically dare him to take me?

I imagine he would never have come over to my house if I didn't tell him to man up. Lord knows male shifters don't like to have their dominance questioned, or at least this has been my experience with the opposite sex.

Now I just feel like a complete idiot.

Don't be sad, Shay. Moon softly whispers.

My sweet, sweet wolf, I'm not sad....

"I'm pissed. Pissed at Foster, pissed that I ever fell for his bullshit, but mostly just pissed at myself." I do not speak this last part through our link. I say this for the whole world to hear. Even though the entire world currently only includes me and my empty house. Regardless, I would say the same thing if I was in the middle of time square on New Year's Eve.

I am a colossal idiot.

Life lesson number four hundred and one: don't believe anything people tell you. Which I should have already known since it is so close to life lesson number two; if given a chance, most people will lie to you. And that warning comes right behind rule number one. Don't trust anyone other than myself.

Epic, colossal fucking fail on all fronts.

The sound of a phone ringing causes me to jump. Scrambling around, I find the phone on the floor, half under my bed, covered by my pants. Seeing them lying there all haphazardly discarded results in another wave of rage ripping through me.

The caller ID reads Finn. Not in the mood to talk to anyone attached to Foster, I toss the damn phone on my nightstand.

Yanking the covers over my head. I can give it back to Ness later today if I see her. If not, I'll give it to Mandy. I'm sure she would be overjoyed to have a reason to chase after him. I'll definitely have to come up with a reason why I have it that doesn't involve Foster, me, and hours of hot sex if I don't want to have to deal with her shit again.

The phone begins ringing again. Unfortunately, the pillow and blankets do nothing to drown out the incessant sound resulting in me snatching it up, fully intending on telling Finch to stop calling until the asshole has his phone back.

"He doesn't have his stupid phone."

Finch does not respond. What I get is open-line silence.

Frustrated, I yell, "So you can stop calling now."

Still no response. I strain my ears. At first, I didn't hear anything leading me to wonder if maybe Finn merely butt-dialed the number while he was sleeping. Yet this thought no sooner materializes when the unmistakable sound of movement eliminates any ideas of this.

"Real mature, Finn," I snap, figuring Foster had him call his phone to find out if he had left it at my place by mistake. Not wanting to play these stupid games, I hang up.

I am just dozing off when the phone rings again. I contemplate throwing the damn thing across my room, but I don't have the money to replace it if it breaks, so I send the call to voicemail. It only takes a couple of seconds before it rings again. Snarling, I have no intention of giving him a chance to say anything as I snap, "Tell him I'll give his damn phone to Ness if I see her later today. If not, he can get it back from Mandy."

Not waiting for a response, I hang up again, and this time I silence the damn thing. By 6:30, I know I am not going back to sleep anytime soon, and there is really no point in lying here.

A flash from his cell has me lifting it to find Finch called ten more times and left a voice message. Maybe he needed to talk with Foster and thought we were screwing around. Sliding my finger over the screen, I'm not surprised to discover the phone is protected, but he does have his emergency contacts set up, allowing me to call Finch back.

His phone rings a couple times before it goes to voice mail. Figuring he kept me awake when he was blowing up this phone with his persistent calling all night, I could do the same to him, so I immediately called him back. This time the phone goes straight to voicemail. Thoroughly irritated, I call Ness.

"What do you want, Foss?" Her voice has the raspy quality of someone who just woke up from a deep sleep.

"Ness—"

"This isn't Foster." She cuts me off. "Who is this? And how did you get my cousin's phone?"

"No, this most certainly isn't Foster—"

Again she cuts me off, "Shay, is that you?"

Sighing, I huff, "Yes, it's Shay. Can you—"

"Why do you have Foster's phone?" her tone turns playful while I am doing my best not to snap at her since she refuses to stop cutting me off.

"Ness, if you stop interrupting me, I'll tell you."

"Lips are zipped," she squeals. I can almost imagine her bouncing on her bed as she lets her mind run wild. I have no intention of telling her the more intimate details of Foster and my time together.

"Foster dropped his phone last night, and I found it." Technically, not a lie. I did find it under my bed, hidden from view by my pants. In my opinion, this constitutes the truth.

Half-truth? Semi-truth?

"I figured if you are going to be around today, I can give it to you." Hmmm, who knew I could come up with such a plausible lie off the cuff.

"Oh, I was hoping—"

Not wanting her to finish the thought of what she was hoping for, I cut her off abruptly, saying, "Nope. Listen, I just thought I should let Foster know I have his phone. If you're busy, he can get it at the bar from Mandy later today, and Finn is trying to get ahold of him."

"Did Finch say what he wanted?"

I want to respond to her question with, 'No, he wouldn't say shit,' but I go with a more diplomatic approach, "No, sorry, he didn't say anything, but he left a message."

*****

Foster

"Foss, is there anything else you want to tell me?" Aunt Claire asks.

I have no idea how to broach this conversation. I imagine it would go something like I met my mate, who I contemplated rejecting because the thought of letting anyone have the amount of control my dad held over my mom terrified me. But after getting to know her, I realize now I can't imagine my life without her in it. When I couldn't stand the idea of her going out with anyone else, I almost tore some poor guy apart before I showed up at her door uninvited. Where I didn't wait for her to tell me what she wanted, instead opting to listen to my wolf and take her. Only to learn more about her shitty life after we made love twice. Oh, and by the way, her dad is the man who saved mom and me when my bastard of a father ordered our death, only to have the sperm donor and useless Alpha kill him for this kindness. Worse, the woman I could easily fall in love with has no damn idea. Yeah, I don't imagine aunt Claire wants to hear all this, so I do not know how to tell her, let alone Shay.

"I will, aunt Claire. I just need to have a conversation with someone first." I figure I owe Shay this. She should be the first person I have this conversation with, but I wouldn't blame her if she didn't want to speak to me again. Hell, I don't want to speak to me. I have never felt so unworthy of someone in my life.

The last thing I need is for Ness to tell her I didn't have pack business this morning, and I spent the morning over here. Excusing myself, I wander back to Ness's room. I rap on the door twice before I hear her say, "It's open."

Walking in, I discover Ness sitting cross-legged on her bed.

115

"Hey Ness, can you do me a favor? If you talk to Shay today, don't tell her you saw me. In fact, don't bring me up at all."

"That's going to be kind of hard since she's on the phone. The one which is currently on speaker," she informs me as she holds up her cell, wiggling it around in the air. "So she totally just heard everything you said, jerk face."

"Don't worry, Foster, I have no intention of looking for you, let alone speaking to you or about you with anyone."

Fuck. Of all times for her not to have that damn phone pressed to her ear, it has to be the one time I open my damn mouth and insert my big fucking foot. This girl is never going to forgive me.

Ness is quick to get off the phone before she begins screaming at me for being such an ass to such a nice girl. I don't say anything because, honestly, she's right. I don't deserve Shay and merit everything Ness is saying to me.

It seems Shay didn't tell Ness about us being together last night. If she had the tongue-lashing Nessie is currently giving me would be so much worse.

Just before she storms out of her room, she barks, "Oh, and Finn is trying to get ahold of you."

"He is?" I begin feeling around my pockets. It doesn't take me long to realize I don't have it; if I had to guess, it is currently with one very pissed-off beautiful blonde who has no intention of talking to me anytime soon.

"He left you a message." I reached out to take her phone. Believing when he couldn't get ahold of me, he left a message on Ness's phone. I already know he didn't come home last night, so he must be at my place.

"What?"

"Come on, Ness, I know I'm an asshole, but seriously."

"Seriously, what? Jackass."

So now I'm a jackass. "Okay, I deserve that. Now, will you please play the message for me, Ness?"

"No."

"No?"

"That's what I said."

"I get you're mad at me, but why make Finn suffer?" One thing can be said about my sweet little cousin... she can be a bear when you piss her off, and right now, she damn near has steam coming out of her ears.

"I can't," she huffs.

"Why not?"

"He left it on your phone, dipshit."

"Can I borrow your phone then?"

"Absolutely not, but I know where you can find yours."

"Come on, Ness, just let me check my messages."

She finally relents and hands me her phone. The instant the voicemail begins to play, I immediately realize the message is not from Finn; it's Max, and his message sends me into a rage.

"We have your pathetic soon-to-be dickless cousin. If you want to see him alive again, I suggest you get your ass out to Cowden's field. I'm sure you know where that is. We'll be waiting. Oh, and Foster, come alone, or your useless fucking cousin will be dead before you get within a hundred yards of him."

Episode Forty-Seven: Dethroning

Foster

FURY RACES THROUGH Shadow and me, hearing Max threatening my cousin. If this asshole believes he has the upper hand by demanding I come alone, he is sadly mistaken. I don't know how many of the '*we*' he referenced may include. It could be two or twenty; either way, it doesn't matter. I will do everything in my power to save my cousin.

I vaguely register Ness bitching at me about Shay, but I don't have time to listen, and I sure as shit can't say anything to her about Finch because she will insist I call in the cavalry. And by cavalry, I mean Ian, Atlas, and Denver.

Jumping into my truck, I expect to find Ness standing on the porch with her hands on her hips; instead, she is yanking the passenger door open.

"What the hell is going on, Foster?"

"Ness, I need to go."

"Then I'm coming with you," she grumbles, slamming the door closed.

"No, you're not," I snap.

"Well, since I'm currently sitting in your stupid truck, I—"

Reaching over, I yank the handle, flinging the door back open. "Get out. Right. Now, Ness."

"What—"

"Now, Vanessa," I growl. Using her given name instead of her nickname makes her realize the seriousness of this situation.

The color bleeds from her face as she slides out of the truck, pausing only long enough to quietly say, "Bring my brother home, Foster."

"I will." Throwing my truck into drive, I know this may be the last thing I say to the cousin I have always thought of as a little sister. There is a genuine possibility that neither of us will be coming home.

I may not be permitted to bring anyone with me, but I am smart enough to recognize a trap and, thankfully, not naïve enough to walk into it blind. I also realize the setup may not necessarily be for me, so I wisely call Atlas to ensure aunt Claire and Ness will be safe.

Fifteen minutes later, I skid my truck to a stop at the chain, which is barring any further progress opting to run the remaining two hundred yards. When I enter the clearing, I discover Max, his band of misfits, and no surprise here, Deacon. I have to admit, the entire drive out here, I suspected he would be a part of this. Seeing him here betraying his pack member for an asshole like Max infuriates me, but not as much as seeing Finch on his knees, bound and gagged with old blood crusted over his face and neck. He must have put up one hell of a fight.

119

"See, dipshit, your cousin does care about the status of your pecker. Just so you know, I was hoping he wasn't going to make it. I wanted to render you a eunuch before leaving you to bleed out."

"Take your fucking hands off my cousin."

Max laughs, lifting his hand up before he lashes out to backhand Finch.

"Or what, asshole?"

"Or I am going to rip your fucking throat out." He laughs again. I can't wait until the day I replace that noise with the sound of him begging.

Neither can I. Shadow roars.

Max turns around to mumble something to the idiot behind him. Meanwhile, I keep my eyes focused on Finch. If we were in our wolf form, we could mind-link so we could plan our attack because make no mistake, I have zero intention of retreating today. Deacon will answer for his actions, and if Shadow gets his way, Max will meet my wolf before the end of the day.

Whatever Finch hears Max saying has his eyes going wide as he struggles against his bonds while muffled sounds escape him. Max smirks at me before he hits Finn, knocking him backward. Since Finch could not brace himself, his head slammed painfully hard against the ground.

"Keep your pathetic comments to yourself," he warns Finch, who is still lying on the ground.

"Are you sure about this, Max?" Deacon asks cryptically.

He levels his eyes on me, the smirk transitioning to a sneer prior to replying, "Yeah, you got this?"

"Your crew knows the deal?"

"Are you doubting my word?"

"No, just confirming." Their polite argument allows me to move closer inch by miserable inch.

"Then they know the deal."

"Then I have this."

"Foster, I can't say it's been a pleasure; however, please enjoy the ass beating my crew plans on providing."

"What…. Too much of a chicken shit to face me, little Maxie?" I taunt, hoping to bring him close enough to prove me wrong. If he takes the bait, he will soon regret it because I will snap his fucking useless neck if his crew doesn't comply with releasing Finch and then back away.

At first, I believe he will take it until he stops and shakes his finger at me before declaring, "I look forward to the next time we are together. I promise you, Foster, I will make you regret those words."

"Just not man enough to do it today?"

A low growl rumbles from the wolf, who wants to break free. As a result, Shadow pushes forward, ready to meet him head-on.

"For all your bluster, you're nothing more than a chickenshit pantywaist." Yeah, that got him. The color of his eyes changes, glowing much brighter than before.

"This is not part of the plan," Deacon yells as he grabs Max's arm.

Max jerks his arm free. "I don't think this will take long."

"I told you Foster is no pushover. He easily took down our last Alpha."

"Maybe your last Alpha was a pussy," Max screams. Spittle flies out of Max's mouth, landing on Deacon's face.

"Yeah, I'm nothing special, but I'm more than enough to take your ass out."

Finch finally comes back up to his knees as he begins his muffled shouts again, desperate in his attempts to tell me whatever he heard. Right now, I can't worry about whatever he heard because I can end this as long as I can get my hands on Max.

"You almost had me, but Nah, I think I'll stick with the plan."

"Running away with your tail between your legs?"

"Someday, very soon, Foster," his warning doesn't mean shit to me. The only thing that bothers me is he is now backing away. "Until then, my crew will have to suffice." He punches Finch, and this time there is no doubt he knocked him out.

Whistling, he circles his finger in the air, indicating his crew should attack. When they rush me as nothing more than mortal human men, I admit a certain satisfaction fills me as I release Shadow to deal with them, knowing he can make short work of this. Just as the first line reaches me, I search the field only to realize Max is gone.

Damn it. I hope Atlas and Denver made it to Aunt Claire's house.

Episode Forty-Eight: Surprise

Shay

*H*EARING HIS COMMENTS further confirms what I already know. For him, last night was nothing more than a challenge I issued. He had second thoughts last night…. While today he regrets everything we did. Maybe Foster should have figured this out before he knocked on my door. Just as I should have stopped it when he first kissed me with those incredibly soft lips.

"Stop that shit right goddamn now, Shay," I chastise myself.

And he smelled heavenly. Moon says dreamingly.

That directive goes for you too, Moon.

I have the afternoon shift at Stooges today, so I jump into the shower, wanting nothing more than to wash his scent off me. Normally when I work this shift, I go in early to help Seamus with stock and setup, and today will be no different. Besides, I need the distraction. Grabbing my stuff, I almost forget his stupid phone. Thank goodness Finch must have gotten ahold of him finally since he hasn't called since earlier this morning.

When I open the door, someone is standing there with their back to me. I don't immediately recognize who it is until they turn. This is when I realize I'm in trouble.

"Hello, Shay."

How the hell does Max know where I live?

"It's not nice not to return a person's greeting."

"Why are you here?"

He clicks his tongue. "You've been a naughty girl."

"What the hell are—" before I can finish, he pounces, slamming something over my mouth and nose. The harder I struggle, the fuzzier everything becomes until the world slips away, leaving only darkness surrounding me.

*****

I have no way of knowing how long I was out, but when I come to, I discover I am tied to a chair in what appears to be an abandoned factory. The floor is covered with not just dust but a thick layer of dirt and debris from the holes dotting the roof.

Not wanting to alert Max that I am awake has me raising only my eyes as I scan the room. When I inspected everything I could, I cautiously lifted my head. The muscles in my neck are stiff from my head hanging the entire time I have been here. Slowly, I look first to the right and then to the left.

The instant my head swings in this direction, I discover Max sitting in a chair, legs kicked up on a rickety table, nonchalantly peeling an apple with a knife that is entirely too large for the task he is completing.

Even though I keep my gaze steady, hoping to portray a sense of calm, collected indifference, secretly I admit if he is trying to scare me, he is doing a fantastic job of it. Slicing off a piece of the apple, he slowly brings it to his mouth. He moves his eyes up to meet mine only after he is finished chewing it.

"Welcome back."

"What are you doing?"

"Currently eating an apple. I thought that would be obvious."

"That's not what I meant."

"Yet it is what you asked."

"O—kay, so allow me to rephrase. Why did you take me?" Placing the apple on the table, he stabs it with the mammoth blade.

"Because I could." Each answer he gives is vague; with these ambiguous responses, I can feel my frustration growing by the second. What I can't sense is Moon. This tells me that in addition to using chloroform, there was a splash of wolfsbane on that cloth too.

"That's not an answer, asshole." I know I probably should have left the snide nickname out of my response; the issue is right now, I just don't give a shit.

"You want an answer. Fine. Initially, I planned to take you, figuring it would throw Foster off his game. When he finds out, I took two people—"

"What the hell do you mean, two people? Who else did you take?" I snap.

He clicks his tongue, then leans the chair back on two legs before continuing as if I never said anything, ".... two people he cares about, he will lose his mind. I'm banking on the fact that he fights for shit when he's pissed."

125

"Who. Did. You. Take?" His smirk continues to grow, as does my rage. The angrier I get, the more adrenaline I have flooding into my system, which is waking up Moon. Turning his tactics against him, I allow a slight chuckle to escape me before I clue this dipshit in on a simple truth.

"If you're banking on him being upset about me, you are in for a world of disappointment because he could care less about me…. or what happens to me."

He laughs, shaking his head. The intention is to display I'm an idiot. Clearly, he doesn't know what I know. This being Foster couldn't wait to get out of my house this morning.

"Yes, because Foster often chases after a guy who asked out one of the waitresses at Stooges." How the hell does he know about this? He wasn't there when it happened.

"If this is what you are hanging your hope on, you're an idiot."

"Even if what you say is true, you should remember I started this conversation by telling you this is why I initially took you. This decision was made weeks ago since then…."

"If you think I have any interest in you—"

He grabs the spot on his chest where his heart should be, although I'm not so sure he has a damn heart, before he dramatically declares, "You wound me, Shay. But no, I am under no illusion you have any interest in me. And after I found out how naughty you have been, I can't say I view you in the same light anymore either."

I can not think of one thing he could be referring to. However, before I can question him further, the clanging of a door being ripped open pulls my attention. My hope is the calvary has come to haul my ass out of this effed-up situation, and right now, I don't even care if the calvary is comprised of only Foster as long as I am free from these ropes soon.

Looking over towards Max, fully planning on gloating, the elation I felt seconds ago melts away as trepidation replaces it when I find him still completely relaxed.

After he finishes chewing another slice of apple, the stupid gloating glare returns. He clears his throat theatrically before snarling, "Shay, I believe you know…." Another door is yanked open, and when I spin this time, I find someone standing there who causes my heart to seize.

"My brother."

Moon is screaming for me to run when we realize who just entered…. Travis.

"Did you really believe you could ever get away from me, bitch? You thought your life was bad before; you haven't seen anything yet." He advises as he storms over towards me, backhanding me the second he is within reach.

Episode Forty-Nine: Challenge

Brady

I DON'T KNOW why Nan's words rattle me so much; nonetheless, they do. I need to do something; anything would be better than sitting around waiting for the worst to come to pass, but where the hell do I begin?

"My handsome little man—"

"I'm not so little anymore, mom," I tell her with an exasperated sigh. She's called me her little man since I was in diapers; one would think she could come up with something better by now, but nope I guess I will forever be her damn little man.

"Semantics. Regardless, come walk with your mom," she replies, looping her arm in mine.

"I'm kind of in the middle of something right now. Raincheck?"

"Since when are you too busy to spend time with your dear old mom? Now come on, I promise not to take up too much of your precious time." Once more, I begin to protest until she silences my objections. She has always been able to manipulate me, and today is no exception.

"You know, my sweet baby boy, I'm not always going to be around, and when I am gone, you'll wish you had taken the time—"

"Alright, mom, a quick walk."

"Wonderful." She leads me out the door into the cool, brisk winter air. Her right arm remains hooked around, mine the entire time while her left hand rests on top of it. She fills most of our walk with meaningless chit-chat. Mostly about me settling down and having pups. Of course, she has her own thoughts on who this woman should be. I'll give you one guess who she believes I should select as my chosen mate.

"Natashia would make a wonderful Luna...." Bet this wasn't too hard for you to figure out.

"...I see so much of myself in her." And this is why she will never be my Luna. In fact, the second I am made Alpha, I think I may claim Shay as my mate just to spite them all.

Well, if I'm being entirely honest, claiming her would not be done merely to spite them. I have always been attracted to Shay and felt a certain pull toward her, but I refused to act on it because I was a chickenshit. I was too damned worried about what everyone would think when I should have only been concerned about her. This is a situation I plan to remedy.

I only have to find her, convince her I mean her no harm, and persuade her to come back to the damn pack who treated her like next to nothing. Prove to her my feelings are real as I try to win her heart and hand, all while keeping her safe until she agrees to be my Luna... if she agrees. If I can accomplish all of this, I will make her mine, and once I claim her, Shay will be beyond their reproach.

"What are you doing, you idiot? You cannot truly be this stupid." My mom's heated words bring me out of my daydreams of Shay, only to find a young she-wolf with her head dropped. I have seen her around before; however, I always had my head shoved too far up my own ass to take notice, let alone learn her name. Damn, I really am a putz.

"I—I'm s—sor—sorry, Luna," she stammers. My mom's wrath is well known throughout the pack, yet this is no way to treat our wolves. Hell, this she-wolf looks like she could hold her own against some of our better sentries. Yet after two sentences from my vicious mother, this proud creature is reduced to a trembling, stuttering mess.

Removing her hand from my arm, I step between them, hoping the expression this scared wolf sees on my face is one of kindness.

"It's okay. You are dismissed."

"Thank you," she quickly says as she bows before she spins and runs in the opposite direction. I wait until she is safely away from us before I turn to look at my mom.

"You shouldn't talk to people like that, mom."

"What? She is barely omega. Certainly not worth the time of her future Alpha."

"She is a member of our pack and, as such worthy of our respect, especially from the future Alpha. After all, it is wolves like her who will help to safeguard this pack, mother. And it would serve you well to remember this."

"Son." She snaps. The tone she is giving me would have had me scampering away as a child. Rushing off to do whatever task elicited this octave, sadly for her, I am no longer a child.

"Mother, if you'll excuse me, I need to return to my previous task, and you should go back to the pack house. Right now, mother." My tone matches hers, and I believe I have left her dumbfounded for the first time ever. Unwilling to wait for her response, I walk away.

Pulling out my phone, I finally know what I need to do to bring Shay home. "Jason, I need a favor, one that can't go any further than the two of us."

"You know I'll do anything for you." My cousin confirms.

"I need to know where all the packs are located in Colorado."

"Why?"

"Can you get the information for me without anyone finding out?" I ask without answering his question.

"Who are you talking to?" He feigns indignation that I could ask something so ridiculous.

"How soon?"

"Give me a day or two."

"Talk to you in two days." Hanging up, I believe I have a solid game plan in place; as long as Shay is still in Colorado, I'll find her, and if I can locate her, I will bring her home. This is my sacred promise to the Moon Goddess and my future Luna.

*****

Foster

I seamlessly shift from the man they apparently believe they would face... to the wolf they will now fight. The instant I release Shadow, he charges the advancing men. Shock and dismay cover their faces, seeing a gigantic wolf cutting through them like they are nothing. However, these men are not who I seek. The one who will soon regret taking one of my family members is currently cowering behind them; the soon-to-be former Alpha, Deacon.

Deacon may believe his only hope of survival is to shift, yet I have no intention of killing him here. He will face his pack for what he has done, and when I kill him like his predecessor, I will do it as a challenge issued for the entire pack to hear as per pack rules.

I still have no desire to be Alpha, so if Ian does not wish to step forward, I will have no choice in the matter. Either way, this asshole, like the one who fathered me and hurt Shay, will no longer have a pack to lead when I am done with them.

Shadow leaps as Deacon's wolf rises to his hind legs. The impact sends him reeling; a howl of pain accompanies the thud. Twisting, I lunge. He rolls just in time to avoid the attack. Surging forward, I slam into his side, which sends him crashing against the ground. Shadow spins, latching down hard on his throat. For a fleeting moment, he struggles, believing he still has the chance of breaking my hold.

His struggle is short-lived as he quickly realizes he never stood a chance against me. He releases one whined cry before he shifts back and raises his hand. It is him submitting to me in the hopes I will release him so he can walk away from this with his life.

"Foster, I never meant.... I didn't.... I wouldn't...."

He tries a different tactic when I do not transition back or release his throat.

"As your Alpha, I command you to release me," he bellows.

Shadow growls, clamping his jaws tight enough to let him know we could care less about a title he is not worthy of. To be the Alpha, you need to be trustworthy, someone who puts the pack before yourself; you need to earn this moniker every day. It is not meant to be wielded like a shield for your own benefit.

"Foster, please. Please don't kill me," he begs.

Shifting back, I replace the jaws crushing his throat with my hand as I inform him, "I have no intention of killing you here, you lousy piece of shit."

"What do you plan to do then?"

"Challenge you," I tell him before I land the punch to knock him out. Finch's muttered words pull my attention from this insignificant prick to the person who originally brought me out here. Striding over to where he is tied up, I pull the gag away first and immediately rethink it.

"Did you have fun?"

"Kicking the shit out of a bunch of dipshits is always a good time."

"I'm not talking about the dipshits."

"Well then, what in the hell are you talking about?"

"You disappeared from Stooge's last night after you chased after a certain blonde-haired, blue-eyed beauty, and somehow she ended up with your phone. So I'll ask you again, did you have fun?" He wiggles his brows as a knowing grin forms on his face. A grin that only serves to piss me off.

"This is what you're worried about," I ask with a grunt while I cut away the last of the ropes which held him. "You're curious about Shay?"

"A man has to have his priorities, cuz, and it seems to me she is a pretty damn good one." He grins as he pulls his arms from behind his back to rub his wrist.

"So tell me, how is it that Shay had your phone, but you were not available to take a call when your favorite cousin was getting the shit kicked out of him?"

"We are not discussing this; however, I would like to hear about why they took you."

"They came looking for you. Deacon wanted you out of the way, but he was pissed that Max was escalating the original time frame," Finch replies as he stands and brushes the debris from his clothes.

"What do you mean?"

"I overheard them arguing the plan was to take you before the next pack meeting. Deacon was going to set you up to take the fall for missing funds he took to front the drug running. Once he convinced the pack you were to blame, he planned on having you trotted out to answer for these falsified claims."

"Smart. If Deacon had proven me to be dishonorable, the pack would never accept a challenge from me to take his role, even if they despise the man."

"Right."

"What I don't understand is why Max would have pushed to move before Deacon was ready."

"Not sure. He only said that he discovered vital information and needed you out of the way sooner." Finn walks over and peers down at a still-unconscious Alpha. "What are you going to do about him?"

"Take him back to the pack." Finch slowly looks over his shoulder toward me. His eyebrows pull together as a puzzled expression covers his face. I do not leave him questioning long....

"So I can challenge him for Alpha."

Episode Fifty: Mistakes

Shay

I INITIALLY BELIEVED discovering Travis standing in the same room as Moon and I could be the most terrifying sight I would ever experience.

I hear a low laugh coming from Max's direction. I can't believe I didn't see the similarities before now.

They have the same eyes... the same personality... hell, even their wolves are similar. But somehow I missed it, and this oversight may cost me my life.

"I can't believe the she-wolf you've been pining for stumbled right into the pack I planned on taking over—"

"I never pined for shit," Travis yells, cutting off Max, whose taunting tone isn't helping my situation.

"What the hell would you call it then, little brother?"

Travis growls before he delivers his clipped answer, "I never had a virgin, and I want her to be my first."

"Hmmm, well then, little brother, you may be woefully disappointed," Max replies as he carves another slice from the apple.

"Bullshit," he growls. When Max just continues to smirk at him, his cocky confidence wavers.

"What are you talking about? What the fuck is he talking about, Shay?" My eyes snap over towards Max, wondering how in the hell he could know about Foster and me.

Travis grabs my hair, jerking my head, so I have no choice but to look at him.

"You will answer me. Have you allowed another to take what rightfully belongs to me?" Spittle splashes my face with each forced word Travis yells.

"Belongs to you? Belongs to you? I never belonged to you." My heated retort is met with a growl from him.

"All you have to do is smell her, brother; his scent is all over her. It clings to her even now. There is only one way for this to linger so potently, even with her vigorous attempts to wash it away this morning. Isn't that right, kitten?" I pull my mouth in a tight line, and my eyes narrow as I pull my brows together. I may refuse to answer Max, but I cannot help the rigid scowl I give him.

"You fucking bitch. I had planned on being easy with you our first time. Now I promise you will feel nothing but pain." He hits me, knocking my gaze from his brother.

"I see you're still as quick-witted as always," Max taunts.

Travis picks up a long discarded metal ball bearing the size of a baseball, heaving it at Max, who merely shifts his head to the right to avoid the incoming missile. The whole time, the confident, cocky grin he has been sporting since I first discovered him never leaves his smug-ass face.

When I first saw him enter the room, I told you I believed Travis being here was the most terrifying thing I could ever witness; this is until I realized what he had been concealing behind his back. It is only then I understand what genuine horror is…. The collar he intends to cage my wolf with.

*****

Foster

As requested, the entire pack is waiting when we arrive at the Alpha lodge. They part to allow me to drive through. Anxiety is beginning to take hold, not for the fight but for the thoughts of what will transpire immediately after.

As per our ways, protocol dictates I have to accept the role or open it for any other who wishes to take the position. The last time I allowed this to happen, we went from bad to worse. I have no desire to lead; truth be told, I am not sure I know how or if I would make a good role model for my people, but all this is a moot point because I cannot allow this to ever happen again.

"Are you okay, Foster?" My cousin asks while placing his hand on my shoulder. Taking a deep breath, I exhale with a nod.

Exiting my truck, I am greeted by Ian. "Foster, is everything okay?"

"Is everyone here?"

"Yes, the entire pack is accounted for." My apprehension rises when I do not see their faces among the questioning ones looking back at me.

"Where are my aunt Claire and Ness?"

"On the porch," he quietly reassures me. I move so that I can get a better view and relief washes over me when I see them flanked by Atlas and Denver. "Those two refuse to leave them, stating they would only vacate their duty when you told them it was okay."

Their unwavering dedication confirms I made the right decision when I sent them. Knowing I can delay this no longer, I open the rear door of my truck, yanking a squirming, hogtied asshole Alpha out, dropping him to the ground in front of the stairs. I do not miss the confused expressions covering my pack member's faces.

"Men and women of the Ash Rock Pack, I called you all here today to bear witness to our Alpha's misconduct. As our Alpha, his priority should be to protect each and every member of this pack. Unfortunately, it has recently come to my attention he is using his title only for his benefit."

Hushed murmurs echo around us as each pack member has an opinion regarding what I just revealed to them.

"What have you discovered, Foster?" One of the younger sentries asks.

"He has partnered with Maximus and is using our pack to not only fund but funnel drugs into the surrounding communities. He does this knowing the risk he puts us all in."

Wanting to ensure I give him the opportunity to dispute the accusations I am leveling at him, I remove his bindings and gag before pulling him to his feet.

"Is this true, Alpha Deacon?" Ian asks.

"No, he's lying. He stole the funds from us, and now he is trying to cover his tracks by redirecting his wrongdoings against me. I have proof; tell them, Betsy. Tell them how he would enter my office after I left."

Betsy's eyes shoot to mine, and I find a desperate plea in them. Knowing Deacon, he holds something over her to ensure the version of events he wants to be relayed to the pack are the ones Betsy tells.

Betsy clears her throat, her discomfort written all over her face having the eyes of her entire pack on her as she slowly begins shuffling her feet.

"You don't need to look at Betsy because I did go into his office. It was the only way I could confirm my suspicions."

"Betsy, to the best of your recollection, whose version of the events is correct?" Betsy looks from me over to Deacon. I witness the brief glare of warning cross his face before he settles it into one of indifference.

Betsy must have seen it too, but whatever reaction he was hoping to elicit is not the one he receives as she straightens her shoulders and confidently declares, "Foster's version is true. Deacon cannot be trusted."

A low growl rumbles through his chest, causing Betsy to sink back from his ire, making me question how much of his temper she has had to face over the years. Yet another reason I should be ashamed of myself for allowing my pack to be run by this inept asshole.

"So what do we do now?" one of the female members of the pack asks.

"You don't have to do anything. I, on the other hand—"

"NO. I won't allow it. You cannot do this to me, you fucking insignificant parasite," Deacon screams.

"Challenge you, Deacon, for the Alpha position of the Ash Rock Pack."

Ian tries to hide his merriment, knowing at long last that Deacon will have to win this pack by fighting the true Alpha.

"I refuse your challenge because you are not worthy enough to run anything, least of all this pack."

"Then you forfeit your title, which passes to Foster immediately." Ian's stern response is met with a vicious growl from the man I plan to depose.

"The fuck you say. I'm not passing shit to him," he snarls as he spits on the ground towards my feet.

"You can't do that—"

"I'm the Alpha. I can do any fuckin thing I want to do," he screams as I remove my shirt and shoes.

"You will face me in the ring, or I will kill you where you stand." My stern proclamation is a promise of what I intend to do. It is now up to him if he will fight back or die as the coward I have long believed him to be.

Ness yells my name, and Deacon takes the opportunity while my back is turned to shift and attack me. His first bite tears through the tendons in my leg. Fisting my hands together, I repeatedly smash them into the nape of his neck until he releases his hold. The instant he does, Shadow is freed.

Moving faster than I thought I would be able to due to the searing pain from the injury inflicted on my leg. The open wound is throwing me slightly off balance. Unfortunately for Deacon, the damage is not enough to help him as I easily avoid his incoming strike. Circling one another, I rapidly gauge his weak points. He leaves his left side unprotected every time he lunges. This is something I can use to my benefit.

Waiting for him to lunge, Shadow swipes his massive paw out, ripping large gashes down the exposed side. Deacon's wolf cries out from the impact and injury left by Shadow. He tries to rush me, but I jump out of his way, twisting to land another hit.

I want nothing more than to teach this asshole a lesson, yet the damage he did with his first bite restricts my movements, affecting my reaction time. When he rears up on his hind legs, I follow suit as we both move in for the killing blow. I am just slightly faster. Biting his snout, he twists, giving me access to the one area he should protect above all others.... his throat.

And this time, I do not intend to allow him to walk away.

The fight ends with a crunch as I rip through flesh and bone. Deacon's limp body falls to the ground, shifting back to his human form for the last time. I allow Shadow time to bask in his victory, but after a few minutes, I change back. Finch appears at my side instantly, holding up a towel I can wrap around my waist as I greet my pack as their Alpha for the first time.

Since I am a man of few words, I keep my speech short, promising to make changes in the pack. I also tell the members that this is not my pack; it's ours. Therefore, I would like to hear their thoughts on the best way forward.

After Twenty minutes and several handshakes and back slaps, I can finally check on my aunt Claire and Ness.

"Are you two okay?" I ask, pulling them both in for a hug.

"Yeah." They answer in unison.

Moving to Atlas and Denver, I shake their hands. I know it is only because of these two they are here safe and sound. Once I have my clothes back on, I advise them I am going to pick up my phone from Mandy.

"Mandy doesn't have your phone, Foss."

"What do you mean?"

"I mean," Ness says dramatically, "I called Stooge's, and Shay didn't take it there."

"What the hell. Isn't that what she told you? She planned on giving it to Mandy." I ask, realizing I may have made a huge mistake sending Atlas and Denver both to my aunt Claire's house.

"Foster, Shay never showed up today for her shift."

Episode Fifty-One: Collared

Shay

I CANNOT DO anything to help settle Moon's pained whimpers and screams of agony. I don't know what's worse, hearing her or realizing I failed her once more since I promised her that it would never happen again after the last time Adela collared us.

Travis grabs my face yanking it up so I cannot look away as he hisses, "Tobias and Adela are going to be so pleased to see you again. I imagine he'll want to reward me for finding the thieving whore who stole the funds for the children's hospital."

"I never stole shit, and you know it. But I'll tell you something I know, either you or Natashia or hell, possibly both of you stole that fuckin money."

The corners of his mouth tip up, which confirms everything I already knew. Even if he does not admit to it, he's the one who took the money. Money meant to help kids afflicted by a horrible disease.

"I suppose I should thank you for taking the fall for that one, Shay," Max calmly tells me. "With the money *you* stole, we had enough to increase our purchase of coke, thereby growing our status within the cartel.

"What the fuck, Max? Why would you tell her that shit? You don't think she isn't going to fucking spill her guts the second I take her back to Tobias."

"So cut her fucking tongue out. It's not like she needs it for anything."

"She needs one to give me head. In fact, I can't wait to feel that tongue of hers sliding over my cock." He further elaborates on this by grabbing his crotch and giving it a good shake. I recoil. Thinking about having his hands on me is bad enough, let alone the thought of that limp dick of his anywhere inside me.

"You're really going to risk sticking your dick inside a mouth filled with teeth. Not very fuckin bright, are you?"

"She'll be an obedient bitch if she wants to keep the fucking collar off, won't you, dog?" He makes the mistake of bringing his face within range, and I do not hesitate to slam my head forward. The crunching of bone and cartilage confirms the assault had the desired effect.

Max's booming laugh as Travis staggers away causes me to jump. "Yeah, I can see how obedient she plans on being."

When Travis falls on his ass, this brings on another bout of roaring laughter from his brother; this time, I can't help joining in.

"Don't worry, little brother, you can take solace in the irrefutable evidence I will give you to prove she is the thief. Then if you still want to stick your dick in her, you can simply take her as your reward. I'm sure your dumbass Alpha will be only too happy to grant you with said gift for returning such a vile, wicked creature."

Max raises his hands, wiggling his fingers in my direction, "Like the boogeyman, this one is."

"You fucking useless bitch," Travis growls as blood drips from between his fingers. Leaping to his feet, he grabs me by the neck, squeezing until not even a molecule of oxygen can get through. I see the strike coming just in time to turn my head, so my nose will not resemble his.

I don't expect to receive any help from Max; he is, after all, Travis's brother and just as big an asshole. The reality of this situation is this: I am going to be returned to the pack who hates me, with indisputable evidence that I stole money I never saw, let alone took, only so this prick can lay claims to my body without actually having to claim me. Not that I would want him to; I would just prefer not to be used and abused for his sick satisfaction.

The thought of what Adela will do to me is almost as disturbing as what Travis has planned. While all of his plans may settle around sex, hers will be all about torture in the worst possible ways. And not just any run-of-the-mill beatings; no, hers is the stuff that nightmares are made of.

I can't imagine they will announce my presence to the entire pack; a select few will be told. The ones who will want to be allowed to participate in punishing me, and they (I'm talking specifically about Natashia) will enjoy every second of it.

I guess this is what I get for daring to dream of a better life. A life free from ridicule, beatings, and servitude. They may be able to make the rest of my life hell, but for a few short months, I knew joy. Moon received her long overdue name and learned what it is like to be a free wolf. This is what they are going to take away from me. Sadly for them, I have experienced it, and I'm not willing to give it up now. So they all better pray they don't drop their guard because I will make them pay if they do. Every. Last. Fuckin. One of them.

"Get her ready for transport," Max advises.

"I need fifteen minutes alone with her," Travis retorts before licking his tongue up the side of my face.

"Fifteen minutes? Seriously? That's all you need? Damn, it doesn't say much for your...." Standing, Max puts his hands in his pockets as he thrusts his hips forward. "Stamina."

"Fuck you, Maximus. We're on a tight schedule."

"Still, if I was sliding into this blonde beauty, I would damn well want to take my time." He blows me a kiss. So they are one and the same. Both are sick, twisted bastards.

My eyes dart around the room, looking for any means of escape. With this damn collar on, I will have no way of shifting, so this removes any hope of help from Moon.

As I previously advised, the factory is a dilapidated, crumbling piece of shit that I have a tough time imagining ever in use. There are windows in here. The issue is they are either too high for me to reach or boarded up. Okay, this leaves little to no escape options, moving on to the next possibility; a weapon.

Don't worry, my sweet wolf. I will get us out of this mess. One way or another, I promise.

Sadly, the only response I receive is her muffled cries. The collar is painful for me but unbearable for her.

Travis bends down to untie the lashings around my ankles. Before he releases me, he warns, "If you kick me, Shay, you will regret it. So you better think long and hard before you do."

I could give a shit less about his damn warning because the second he releases me, I plan to slam my foot into his face as hard as I can.

One leg down.... I can feel a slight tingling beginning to build just under my skin.

Second leg freed.... It is the feeling you get when you are preparing to run for your life or fight for it.

Right arm no longer restrained.... Only one more left. I fully intend to take matters into my own hands the instant he releases it.

Travis is halfway through untying the rope holding my last limb in place. For the first time since I opened that door, I believe something may actually go my way until his wicked eyes come up to meet mine. They shimmer for the briefest of seconds before he slams a four-inch blade deep into my thigh.

"Just in case you have any grand plans of escape." I can't imagine the scream I released could have gone unheard if anyone was around here.

Slicing the last of the ropes away, he yanks me up but leaves the blade firmly embedded in my leg. Before I have any chance of fighting off this miserable prick, he has me tossed over his shoulder, heading further into the factory.

"Hey asshole, the exit is this way."

"And I told you I needed fifteen minutes." Hearing he fully intends on going through with his attack, I thrash my body back and forth, praying I can break his hold on me.

"I've been waiting for this for a fucking long time, and as promised, I have no intention of being gentle."

Episode Fifty-Two: Searching

Foster

I WOULD HAVE preferred to do this alone, but Finch and Ness insisted on coming with me. As a matter of fact, Ness dove into the back of my truck and refused to get out. This is why I now have the cousin I have been trying to protect all day riding along as I try to find my missing mate.

Skidding to a stop at Stooge's, I jump out of the truck, not even bothering to close the door. Rushing inside, I am greeted by an overtly happy Mandy.

"Where's Seamus?"

"He's busy, but I can help you with," irritation springs to life as I watch her gaze slide over my body, "anything you need."

"I need Seamus. Now, where in the fuck is he?"

"The—" she doesn't finish her sentence before he comes storming out of the kitchen.

"Houl yer whisht, boy. Yer actin the maggot, ya bloody egit."

"Seamus, I need to speak to you," I tell him but elaborate when I see all the eyes in the bar focused on me. "Alone."

"Foster, is this about Shay?" Hyde asks. I know he cares about her and has looked after her since she moved here, which makes me feel bad about keeping this from him. Regrettably, I need discretion, and the more people who know, the less secrecy I retain.

"Seamus, please." I know my beseeching tone does nothing to help calm Hyde's anxiety.

"Aye, follow me." He leads me through the kitchen and out a door at the backside of the building. I can barely distinguish the chimney from the house Shay has been renting from this vantage point.

"Is tichy okay?"

"Tichy?"

"Shay," he says in a huff.

"I don't know. That's why I'm here. When did you see her last?"

"Last night when you chased after 'er like yer arse was on fire."

"She didn't come in today at all? Not even to give Mandy my phone?"

"No, not a titter of wit the likes of them. Fighting over a bloke who from where I'm standin' only seems to care for one of 'em. At least, this is me hope."

Without answering his question, I rush to the front of the bar to retrieve my truck. A few minutes later, I skid to a stop in front of her house. I'm praying we can find something that will lead me to her.

Ness, Finch, and I each begin searching. At first glance, this place appeared to be in order, nothing amiss; however, with our heightened sense and Shay's scent still clinging to my clothes, I knew someone else was here.

And not just any someone, the same asshole who took Finch.

A low growl rumbles deep in my chest as I snarl, "Max."

Ness's eyes widen as her head whips around. She must think I said it because I saw him. Finch, however, seems to understand immediately.

"He was the one who came here?"

"Yeah," the answer is a roar from not just me but Shadow as well.

We all begin surveying the area, searching for any clues as to where she could be or why he would come here. Yet, with every passing second, the cold hard reality is becoming impossible to ignore. Shay was his intended target all along, not aunt Claire or Ness.

What I don't understand is why he would want her; I realize I didn't use the best judgment last night, but shit, there is no fuckin way he or Deacon could have found out that quickly or known how much she means to me. Which indicates he wanted her for another reason. I guess this is also what had him pushing up the time frame for Deacon to face me.

"Anything?" The quiver in Ness's voice confirms the unease we are all feeling.

"No."

"Didn't you claim her last night?" Ness's intrusive question pisses me off. This is the last thing she should be worried about.

"Knock it off, Vanessa. This is neither the time nor the place."

"Don't you Vanessa me, Foster Brannon. I was asking because if you had, your mate bond would be increased significantly, meaning you could use it to track her, you idiot."

Reaching out, I pull Ness into my arms to hug her as I tell her, "You're a genius, Nessie."

My compliment must make up for the slip-of-a-tongue reference to the monster again. Knowing I cannot shift out here on her front porch in broad daylight, I rush into the woods and tell Foster to track me with the truck. I promise him I will stay just inside the tree line.

Within minutes of shifting, Shadow picks up the anguished cries from Moon. A surge of emotions fills me as his cries and howls mimic hers. Every whimper is directly related to a whine from Moon, every growl a reaction to her feral screams as pain consumes her.

While Shadow is focused on Moon, I am sensing Shay's emotions. They batter against my mind, wrap around my heart, and squeeze painfully. From her concern for what is happening to Moon, her pain from whatever Max is doing to her, to Shay's prevailing emotion, which is one of terror. They are all-consuming, and I know I must get to her soon.

Pushing Shadow harder than I ever have before. We race through the woods, unaffected by the low-hanging limbs slapping his muzzle, the rocks biting into his paws, or the fallen branches ripping at his fur. No, none of these things matter, as his only thought mirrors my own....

Save Moon, save Shay, save mate.

With every stride, I feel us moving nearer to her. Reducing the distance separating us and bringing me one step closer to killing the bastard who took her.

*****

Brady

"You're sure just these two packs?"

"Yep, just Ash Rock and Whispering Winds. From what I'm hearing, they're sister packs. So more than likely, whatever one pack knows, the other will too. Now that you have your information, mind telling me why you wanted it? This wouldn't have anything to do with that she-wolf who stole from our packs, would it?"

"Thanks," I reply without giving him the answers he seeks. He's smart…. Well, smart enough he should be able to figure it out on his own with enough time. I just pray not too quickly since I want to ensure I find her long before they begin searching.

Not wanting to waste any time, I throw a few things into my duffle bag. If anyone sees me leaving, with any luck, they will think I am heading over to my uncle's pack, White Fang, for another training session. Grabbing all the cash I have on hand, just over a thousand dollars, I don't want to leave a paper trail they could follow by using my credit cards or bank card.

I rush down the hall towards the exit and find Maggie knocking on my office door. At least someone understands proper protocol when you encounter a closed door. Her head whips in my direction when she hears me approaching.

"Brady, do you have a minute?"

"I'm just on my way out."

"Have you gotten any further in your investigation?" she asks hesitantly in a low tone as her eyes dart around the hallway, searching for any curious observers.

"No, not yet. Listen, I really need to get going."

"You.... You found her, didn't you." Her hand on my arm stops me temporarily.

"Don't have any idea what you're talking about. I'm just going for training," I tell her as I readjust the strap on my bag.

"Bullshit," she snaps, causing me to whirl around on her. Realizing her mistake, she cringes away from me. "What I meant to say is I'm worried about her too. So I'm asking you to please tell me if you found her, Brady."

Inspecting her face for any hint of a lie. I realize I would never have gotten this far without her help. "Alright, yeah, I have my suspicions about where I might find her, although I don't know her exact location."

"Is that where you're going?" She asks, picking up her pace to stay next to me as I continue towards my truck. "If you are, then let me come with you."

"No. No, damn way am I going to put you at risk." I tell her, knowing what I will face if my dad finds out I discovered her location and did not inform the rest of them. Maggie would not get off as easily.

"Brady, if you find her, she'll never believe you, nor will she come with you willingly. Maybe I can convince her that you mean her no harm. But I can only do that if you take me with you."

"Grab a few things, and let's go." Maggie turns to run to her room as I further tell her. "Oh and Mags.... Don't let anyone see you leave."

Episode Fifty-Three: Locating

Shay

TRAVIS THROWS ME down on the only piece of furniture left in the room; a warped desk. Which is leaning to one side because there are only two remaining working legs to hold it upright. He rips my shirt open only to find another underneath it, resulting in a low growl.

Bending over, he viciously bites down on my breast. I can't stop the scream tearing through me from the unwanted contact and the indescribable pain he is exacting.

"No time to waste on foreplay." He slams himself between my legs, grinding against me as he rips the tattered remains of my shirt away.

I throw my hands out, striking him as hard as possible, which only angers him further. His response is immediate, and I have no time to block or defend myself as white light clouds my vision from the punch he landed.

Groaning, I roll my head, trying to clear the confusion and bring my eyes back into focus. Moon's cries have morphed into a guttural howl as she realizes what he intends to do. With one hand, he pins my arms over my head while the other clamps painfully around my throat.

"That will be the last time you ever fucking hit me. Do you understand me, you worthless bitch?" Worthless. This asshole has the nerve to call me worthless while he is grinding himself against me as he prepares to rape me. Even if I wanted to respond, I can't because he is currently crushing my vocal cords and the airways needed to take in precious oxygen.

Seeing my lack of response as a refusal to speak as opposed to the reality, which is the inability to respond, he moves his leg over and slams it against mine. The issue is I still have the knife he embedded there stuck in my leg, so the action drives it further into my thigh, further severing muscles and arteries.

I hate that I give him the satisfaction of seeing the pain he caused. I may not be able to physically scream, but my mouth falls open as a strangled, silent shriek erupts. He slams his head forward. He finds his mark, and tears instantly fill my eyes as I feel my nose shatter from the impact.

Travis is winning, and there is nothing I can do to stop him.

After several more long, painful seconds without being able to breathe, he finally releases my throat so he can flip me over on my stomach. He shoves my head against the desk as he rips my jeans down, dislodging the knife in the process.

With the weapon gone, the blood, which was only seeping from around the blade, is now free to flow from the open wound, soaking my leg in thick, coppery liquid. One might think this would stop him, but it has no effect as I listen to the sound of him unbuttoning his jeans.

155

"Don't do this, please," I beg. I know there's no point Travis could give a shit less if I beg or plead or pray to the Goddess or promise him the world. This sick, twisted bastard gets off on this and has no intentions of stopping.

I cry out as I feel him rubbing the head of his penis over my exposed vagina. It will only be a matter of seconds before he slams inside of me, and if he does, I don't know if I will ever be the same girl again. Pawing frantically at the hand holding my head in place, I shift my hips before slamming my foot up.

He howls as I land a direct blow to his manhood. I struggle to break free, knowing this is my last chance to save myself. He throws me aside, sending me headfirst into the brick wall. The impact is jarring; as much as Moon screams for me to run, I can't seem to make my legs comply as darkness overtakes me.

*****

Foster

Her fear is palpable; it surrounds us the closer we get. Shadow surges forward using every ounce of strength left in him, moving faster than I knew was possible. I contemplate holding him back, knowing I will need something left in me once we arrive.

I am only vaguely aware of the truck trying to keep track of me as I zoom through the brush and the overgrowth.

The instant the factory comes into view, I know she's in there, and I know she's not alone. I am not afraid of facing whoever I may discover in there, nor am I afraid of killing them.

What has dread pooling low in my abdomen is the fear of what condition I will find her in.

Finch floors the gas pedal so he can catch up with me. By the time I arrive at the building, Finch is already behind me in his wolf form. Busting through the door, which is already in shambles, I release a growling howl to let her know I'm here.

*****

Shay

My eyes flutter open only to see Travis stalking toward me, his genitals protectively cradled in his cupped hand.

"You fucking little bitch," he spits as he brings his foot up and kicks me. His intended target is my face, but I turn it at the last possible second, causing his foot to land on the side of my head. If this wasn't bad enough, the force from the assault sends my head crashing into the brick wall I am collapsed against.

"Game time is over!" He snarls.

The next words I hear are like music to my ears.

"Time's up. Foster found us, and he's not alone," Max yells as he bursts into the room Travis is holding me in.

Travis runs forward, grabbing my upper body to toss me over his shoulder, but when I unexpectantly buck, he loses his grip on me, sending me to the ground in a crumpled heap.

"Leave her," Max commands as he heads to the other exit.

"I am not leaving her behind," Travis hisses, trying again to pick me up. With my pants still pulled down below my knees, I don't have many options.

157

Except this... Rearing back, I kick out at him, landing my feet squarely against his chin and spraying blood from the knife wound in a wide ark around me; the action also sends him stumbling away from me.

"You will if you want to live because, trust me, when he discovers what you just tried to do to her, he will kill you, and neither one of us will be able to stop him. I don't plan on dying here today because you wanted to get your dick wet. Now move it, baby brother." Max doesn't wait for a retort as he grabs Travis by the shirt and pulls him out of the room.

As happy as I was when Max broke through that door, the next thing I hear is the best sound I could imagine. It is the sound of Shadow coming to save Moon, and her whimpered cries confirm she knows it too.

Episode Fifty-Four: Darkness Falls

Shay

REALIZING THE SHAMBLES he left my clothes in, I try desperately to cover myself. I know there is nothing I can do about my shredded shirt, so I frantically begin pulling my pants up, hoping to cover up at least some of what almost happened.

The pain in my leg has my vision blurring, and I am afraid I may pass out long before I can get the jeans soaked with my blood back in place. My muscles are aching, my head is pounding, and my thoughts are fuzzy from blood loss. I barely manage to slip my jeans over my hips before every ounce of strength I have is depleted. I know if I could remove this damn collar, Moon could aid me with healing. Regrettably, I don't know how to take it off, nor do I have anything left in me to even try.

Foster burst through the door just as I slumped to the ground. He looks almost otherworldly, standing there with his eyes ablaze, his skin shining from the sheen of sweat covering it and the golden sunlight streaming around him, lighting him up as if he is some ethereal being.

My reluctant knight in shining armor, the knight who told me in no uncertain terms that he did not want to hold this position, yet this is the second time someone has forced him to take on the role.

When his eyes settle on me, taking in my disheveled state, he sprints through the same door Max and Travis went out not more than a few moments before. I have no illusion of grandeur; I never expected him to rush to my side and scoop me into his arms, yet I cannot help the hurt my heart experienced knowing he was only doing what he must.

My heartbreak is swiftly replaced with embarrassment when Finch enters. With my shirt shredded, my breasts are still out on full display. His face shifts from one of concern to one of fury, but I do not miss the pity clouding his eyes.

Pity.... I hate this emotion, and I despise having anyone look at me as someone who needs it. I can handle hate, disgust, indignation, superiority, and even sadness, but pity... is something I cannot. His sympathy strips me bare even more than having Travis remove my clothes because his pity demolishes the walls I have carefully built and leaves this sad, pathetic girl exposed for the world to see.

Hoping to remove his pity-filled gaze from me, I cover my breast from his view; my breath catches as I try to hide more than my naked frame. I close my eyes and turn my head, not wanting him to see the pain covering my face.

One blessed moment later, Ness is beside me, cradling me in her arms as I hear Finch exit the room. Ness pulls off her jacket to wrap around me, granting me the slimmest semblance of dignity back.

Hot tears burn my eyes not because of what happened, not because some asshole tried to force himself on me, not because I have a huge seeping gash in my leg from said asshole, but because the people I care about, the ones I had hoped I would call friends, found me like this. I hate appearing weak, and this right here, this is almost as weak as I could ever feel.

"Shay, I'm sorry this happened." She sniffles. Further driving home, I am now someone they all pity. I'm that girl. I think I prefer being invisible.

Pulling away from her, I try to stand, but my limbs will not cooperate, and the attempt causes the wound to reopen as a river of blood resumes flowing down my thigh. Looking down at the jeans, now permanently stained crimson, I wonder how much more blood I can lose before the world crumbles away from me.

At some point, while I was watching the blood, I must have passed out because the next thing I am conscious of is being in the back seat of Foster's truck. Panic instantly replaces confusion as I think back to the last time I was in here and the memory of how neat and clean he keeps the inside, the inside I am currently bleeding all over.

Moon has gone silent, which has a fresh fear filling me. With a shaky hand, I discover the collar is still firmly encased around my neck. I need to tell them to take it off me. If they do, I can shift, allowing Moon the opportunity to heal me. Trying to sit up so I can tell them, I ultimately give up and let the sweet serenity of darkness consume me once more.

*****

I am only vaguely aware of someone carrying me. Whoever this person is, smells so wonderful, and strong, and inviting. I want nothing more in this world than to curl into whomever it is and stay here until Moon beckons me to run with her again.

Did I just sigh?

Shit. Whoever has me definitely had to hear it. I feel embarrassed, but the heat that normally accompanies this emotion, the heat that brightens my cheeks, does not come.

Huh, I wonder why.

Softness replaces the hard lines of the body that held me moments ago. I instantly miss the smell. I want the hard lines back. Nothing bad could ever happen to me held against such a solid frame.

Moon, can you bring it back? The scent, the body, the safety? Moon?

Moon, can you hear me?

Shame, she must be just as tired as I am.

It's alright, my sweet wolf. You rest; maybe after we wake up, you can help me find whoever it belonged to.

*****

Foster

When I discovered Shay crumpled on the floor, blood coating the ground around her, her shirt missing, pants barely pulled up, I lost every ounce of control until the only thought that remained was of making Max pay for doing this to her.

I knew he was not alone because my wolf picked up another male's scent. I don't give a shit. I could care less if he has the entirety of every rogue at his back; I plan to hunt him, find him, and kill him for doing this to her.

And I will not rest until we see this task done. I will give Shay the solace of knowing he can never hurt her again. Why the hell does the Moon Goddess continue to permit this gentle and beautiful soul to suffer as she has.

I chased them until they crossed the state lines. It was only then I heard Finch screaming for me to stop. That we needed to go back, that Shay needed help. As much as Ness would want to rush her to the pack healers, there is no way she could carry her, and absolutely no fuckin way she would be able to lift Shay into my truck.

Shadow whimpers upon finding her unconscious, surrounded by more blood than a body should be able to lose and still live, but we can feel her heartbeat while it is weak; I can still detect it.

"Why is her wolf not coming out to heal her?" Finch asks as he squats next to her.

"She's collard."

"What?" Ness cries as she puts her hand to her mouth while Finn reaches out to touch the thing but wisely pulls his hand back just shy of it. This is not a practice they have had to endure and something I have only ever heard of. I didn't realize this unique form of torture was still carried out.

"Take it off her," Ness begs.

"I'm not sure if it's safe just to rip it off. We need to talk to someone with more knowledge than I have." I tell them, knowing if I have any hope of seeing her smile again, I need to get her help. Trying not to start the torrent of blood from the wound on her leg to begin again, I tie the scraps of her shirt high on her thigh before I gently pick her up.

Startled to find her already porcelain skin is absent of any color, the urgency of this situation becomes all too real.

Shadow senses each time her hazy mind tries to bring her out of the deep slumber she has sunk into.

I would prefer to have her at my cottage, but the healers are closer to the Alpha lodge, so this is the best place I can take her. The place where she will receive the medical attention she needs.

Carrying her limp body into the house, I know she's still with me when I hear her inhale deeply. In her confused oxygen-starved state, she still recognized me. I pray our mate bond can offer her the strength her own body lacks.

"You need to get that thing off her." Ness's demanding tone has both the healers stepping away from her.

"We—we don't... don't know how." They stammer. I had hoped they would know, but it makes no difference because there is one other soul I am aware of who may possess the knowledge we seek, and I waste no more time as I pull my phone from my pocket.

"Who are you calling?" my aunt Claire asks. She met us at my truck door after Ness called her on the drive back to pack land, hoping she could help.

"The only person who may know."

It is not our way of taking pack business outside the pack, but right now, I could give a shit less about procedures. The phone rings twice before I hear his gruff voice.

"Shay needs your help."

My voice is thick with the emotions swirling within me; he realizes the seriousness of my call. He confirms he is on his way, but to make sure he understands the dire circumstances we all face, I elaborate with, "I think she may be dying."

My eyes come up to meet my family as I finish, "You need to hurry…. Seamus."

Episode Fifty-Five: Knight

Shay

*W*HEN I FINALLY wake up, I haven't the foggiest idea where I am. Thankfully, I find a familiar face attached to the sleeping body in the chair next to the bed I am recovering in. Ness.

My throat hurts, my muscles ache, my thigh is throbbing, and Moon is still sleeping.

Why would she still be sleeping this late in the day? Shaking my head to clear the grogginess that only comes from a deep sleep. The memory of the collar clamped around my neck has me jerking upright as my hand flies to my throat.

Gone.

Someone removed it. Moon is still alive, which answers why she is still sleeping; she needs to recover.

It may be gone, but the damage inflicted while I wore it will remain just like last time.

"Welcome back to the land of the living," I hear Ness yawn. Looking over my shoulder at her, I watch as she stretches her arms over her head and readjusts in the chair, trying to find a more comfortable position.

"Thanks."

"You gave us all one hell of a fright."

"I kinda gave myself one too," I confess as the lingering haze lifts, revealing more memory from my time with Max and Travis. I know I was extremely close to dying in that factory. But Ness, Finch, and, unbelievably, Foster came to rescue me.

"How are you feeling?"

"Like I was run over by a truck that decided to shift into reverse to make sure he completed the job fully."

"Ouch."

"Yep. How the hell did you find me?"

"Ummm, I.... Actually, you're asking the wrong person."

"You were there. I can't imagine anyone else could answer it better than you." She smiles at me but refuses to give me what I seek. I figure she is hinting at Foster but doesn't want to actually say this is who I need to talk to since, let's face it, Foster and I didn't leave things on the best of terms.

"Alright then, can you at least tell me where I am?"

"Sure, our pack Alpha house."

Throwing the covers off, I scramble out of bed, my breath coming in short, clipped gulps.

"Why in the hell would you bring me here? I'm rogue, Ness. Your Alpha would be within his rights to kill me."

"I don't think you have to worry about that," she says with a grin normally reserved for times when you know a secret about the person you're talking to, but I have no idea why she would be giving it to me.

"You can't know that, Ness. You do not know what it's like to be rogue nor how your Alpha will respond to me being here when he finds out."

With the same knowing grin covering her face, she absentmindedly mutters, "Ummm, no, I'm pretty sure I know exactly how he will respond."

"I shouldn't be here. I should go now," I tell her, looking around for my clothes.

"Wait, don't rush off just yet." Ness stands and walks toward the door as my eyes continue to search for my missing clothes. The wound in my leg has changed from a low throb to extreme pain from the sudden movement after however long I have been immobile.

"Promise me you won't leave until I come back." Since I don't have any clothes, not to mention I kind of owe it to her not to leave. Without Ness, I wouldn't be here, so I figure this is the least I can do. Nodding, she opens the door to go but pokes her head back in to tell me, "Oh, and there's something on the dresser for you."

Hobbling over, the only thing I find is a cell phone. All doubt is removed that this is the 'something' she was referring to when I touch the screen and see my name appear on it.

After checking out the cell phone for an indeterminate amount of time, I'm done playing and beginning to wonder where the hell Ness has gotten to. Sneaking out into the hall, I look left and right. This place is amazing, nothing like the Alpha house from my pack.

It's open and airy, bright and cheerful, but most importantly, there is no lingering sense of trepidation that hangs heavy in the air like at Tobias and Adela's home. Wandering from one picture to the next, I can't help but marvel at the smiling faces staring back at me. She pulls my attention when I hear Ness talking to someone she is obviously unhappy with.

"I don't understand. Why not?"

"I've already told you."

"That's not a reason, Foster." Foster? Shit, I shouldn't be listening to this. I begin backing away slowly until I hear him growl.

"I am not claiming her as my mate, so drop it, Ness. This has to stop. I'm not going to keep doing this shit... I can't be the knight in shining fuckin armor you're hoping for." Even though I already knew as much, I admit that hearing him say the words is every bit as painful as the damage inflicted by Travis. Especially since we all know the 'she' he is referring to is me.

I never asked him to claim me as his mate, and I certainly don't expect it. What I really don't understand is why everyone else has to get involved with this.

His statement also tells me one other thing, something he doesn't actually say, but the meaning comes through loud and clear. He has no desire to keep pulling my ass out of trouble.

I've got news for him; I never asked him to be my knight. I don't need a knight, and I certainly don't want one. Specifically, one who obviously doesn't want to be in the same room, let alone share their life with me.

"So fuckin done with this," I growl as I decide I've wasted enough time here and around this self-centered asshole.

Yeah, I called him self-centered because he never took into consideration what I wanted, only what he thought I desired. Maybe if he had asked, I could have told him I didn't want shit from him. Least of all, him claiming me as his godforsaken mate.

*****

Somehow I managed to slip out of the house and off their pack land without being spotted or chased. Although I will admit my legs were shaking the entire time. Someone really needs to talk to them about security.

Not this someone.

Maybe Mandy. I'm sure she could give him pointers on how to beef up their defenses.

I'm better than halfway home when the phone I forgot I was holding begins ringing. I glance down, finding the last name I want to see right now, Foster.

Well, eff him, he doesn't want to be a knight, and I don't have any plans of being a doormat. If he is the one who bought this damn thing, I will happily return it so he doesn't think he has an open-door invitation to call me whenever he wants. Clicking the red phone button, I send his ass to no man's land.

The closer I get to my house, the more my nerves start to get to me. Every noise I hear is Travis or Max or both of them coming to cart me away again. I wish Moon was awake. Listening to her voice would help calm my racing thoughts and pounding heart.

Cautiously sneaking around the front of my house, my eyes scan the street, looking for anything out of the ordinary. There's a truck parked in front of the house next to mine. I can make out the shapes of two people. My heart rate spikes until I realize one of them is definitely female, eliminating the possibility of these individuals being Max and Travis. Still, I use extreme care, ensuring I stay within the shadows as I slip onto the porch before rushing into my house.

Once inside, I lock the doors tightly before peeking through my curtains. I search for any signs of movement on the street or the tree line across from my house. I nearly jump out of my skin when the cell phone I keep forgetting I have rings.

I need to take several deep breaths before I pull the damn thing out of my pocket, fully prepared to send Foster's ass to voicemail until I see it's Ness calling. I hate being an ass to her, so unlike my refusal to answer Foster's call, I pick up for her.

"Hello?"

"Shay, why did you leave? I told you the Alpha—"

"I didn't leave because of the Alpha; I left because...." What I want to say is that I know when I'm not wanted, but this would only be true if I was referring to Foster, "I was ready to come home."

"So why didn't you answer when Foster called?"

Once more, I could go with the truth here and tell her I don't want to talk to the man who thinks of me as little more than a one-night stand irritant, but diplomacy wins out yet again, "I guess I didn't hear the phone when he called."

"Oh good," she says with an exaggerated sigh of relief, "Just hang on a minute while I get him."

"What? No." I say in a rush.

"Why?"

"I'm tired. I'm just getting ready to go to bed. I'll talk to your cousin another time."

"My cousin? When did Foss become just my cousin—"

"You have a good evening, Ness." I hang up before she can say anything else, and to ensure I will not have an onslaught of calls, I power off the phone. I have no desire to hear it ringing all night.

When I clicked off the light, a soft knock at the front door echoes through the room. Remembering what happened the last time I opened this door, I briefly contemplate calling

171

Foster's phone. Why call him when I've already said I don't want a knight?

Simple, I am hoping I will hear it ring from my front porch, but this thought is only fleeting since he has made it clear he doesn't want to keep pulling my ass out of the fire, and if I call him, he will feel obligated.

Inching closer to the window, I glance out. I relax the instant I realize whoever is out there is undeniably female. I can handle a female, but two crazed shifters, not so much.

Still erring on the side of caution, I grab the bat I have sitting next to the door. Had I known what I would find when I opened it, I would have gotten something much bigger than a bat.

"Hello, Shay."

"How the fuck did you find me, Brady?"

Episode Fifty-Six: Truth in Words

Shay

*A*FTER A WHOLE lot of promises that they are not here to haul me back to the pack, I finally relent and let Brady and Maggie into my house. He made small talk about how nice my place is, how good I look, and my personal favorite, what a nice little life I have created for myself here.

Without a doubt, it is… a nice little life. Well, except for a mate I wish would suddenly decide to pack up and hit the road. But aside from this one little minor irritant, my life is extremely nice. It is better than I ever hoped for and vastly better than anything they offered me. I'm sure it's insignificant to them, but to Moon and me, it's everything we ever wanted… minus the mate.

But I was utterly unprepared for what he said after the civilities.

Marcelle Valentine

"I know you didn't steal the money, Shay, or the necklace for that matter. I also acknowledge that you weren't treated the best by me or anyone else. I'm hoping I can make that up to you. I'm here to ask you to come back with me to the pack."

"What? NO! There is absolutely no damn way I will ever go back there."

For the next twenty minutes, he tells me all the reasons why I should come back, the direction he wants to take the pack in, and how my presence can help him achieve these goals. As much as I wish I could say he's lying, I can't because I believe he is nothing like Tobias or Adela. I think he truly wants his pack to be a better place for all the wolves there. Besides the fact that I like my life here, there is another reason I can't go back there, Travis.

"Are you going to protect me from Travis?" The second the words leave my mouth, I instantly regret them.

"Is he the reason you ran, the one who did all this to you?" His eyes roam the still-healing bruises covering my face and neck.

"If I told you he was the one who did all this, would it matter? Because It never did before." Brady is out of his seat and kneeling before me, my hands firmly held in his. His eyes are filled with what I can only imagine is anger. I recoil, afraid he plans to punish me for speaking such atrocious things about his best friend and future Beta, yet what he says next shocks me to the core.

"If he ever shows his face around the pack again, I'll kill him. I promise no one will ever hurt you again, Shay."

"The Luna—"

"No one, not even my mom and dad. I swear to the Moon Goddess I will protect you no matter what anyone thinks. No

174

matter what anyone says. No. Matter. What, Shay. I will make up for every second of pain my pack and I have caused you. My ceremony to take over as Alpha is next week, and I would like nothing more than to have you standing next to me during it."

"Pack members are not permitted—"

"Not as a pack member but as my chosen mate. As my Luna." I pull back. I know my shock is clear. Hell, I can feel it splashed across my face.

"I never wanted to be Luna."

"I am not asking you because I think you want to be the Luna for our pack; I'm asking you because I can think of no one better to stand next to me. No one better to evoke genuine changes in our ranks. To be honest, there is no one else I want at my side or as my chosen mate."

"I don't think I would make a very good...." I trail off, confused by everything he is saying and about his abrupt change in heart. What if this is all just a ruse to get me back there? I would like to see Nan. I miss her more than I care to admit. But if I go back and they collar me, I don't think Moon could ever survive another instance of the collar that has hurt her so much.

"He's telling you the truth, Shay. Brady has been looking for you since right after you went missing. When he realized everything they were saying about you was a lie." Maggie, my best friend. While she may not have stopped them when they hurt me, she never outright lied to me, and I have no reason to believe she would start now. Furthermore, something in his eyes confirms everything he is saying; all the words I longed to hear months ago are true. He wants me to come home, and more than this, he wants me to stand next to him as his equal.

But my heart and Moon both want someone else. Sadly, his desire lies elsewhere. I don't know of anything that could be worse than watching the person you love find happiness with another. Lifting my eyes, I begin to accept until this reality hits me.

"You have a fated mate out there somewhere, and when you find her, your heart and soul will forge an unbreakable bond with hers. You will know what it means to have found your other half."

"Then I hope she has found what I have and stays wherever she is. Come home with me, Shay. Allow me the chance to show you what you mean to me. Let me make amends for what we did to you all these years."

My life here plays out in my mind pining for a man who doesn't want me, who would have preferred I never came. For him, our bond is not all-consuming. It's little more than a nuisance, one he would be only too happy to be rid of.

I know my life shouldn't be decided by something as trivial as this, but I am no longer willing to hurt Moon, and being here, this close to her mate without being able to spend time with him, is every bit as agonizing for her as the collar is. She doesn't deserve to feel like nothing, and I won't allow it any longer, even if it means leaving behind the life I could have had so maybe she can have the life she always should have.

I feel her trying to wake up. More than anything, I wish she would. I want to know how she feels about staying here if Shadow is no longer an option. Going back to my old pack feels like I'm losing ground. A huge mammoth step backward. If I do go back, will I be crushing the parts of me I am only now discovering?

I'm torn. My head and heart are at war with one another.

Stay or go.
This is the choice I must make.

*****

Foster

After Shay left the Alpha Lodge so abruptly and refused to answer my calls, I decided to give her some space. A chance to heal before I punch another hole in her chest to rip her heart out when I tell her the truth.

She deserves to know; she should be told her dad's choice was not wasted. That I will live the entirety of my days making sure I honor the man who allowed me to be here. Granted me a life my own father sought so hard to end.

Maybe then she will understand why I will never be worthy of her. Why I cannot claim her as my mate, regardless of how much my heart and wolf desire this.

This is why I'm at my aunt's house seeking out my cousin's help. I know if anyone can get her to talk to me, Ness can.

"I haven't seen or talked to Shay since the day she left the Alpha Lodge. Thanks for that, by the way."

"I'm not following."

"Because of you and your damn inability to grow a pair, I lost one of my best friends."

"Really, Ness, grow a pair?"

"What? I've heard you and Finn say it before, and it seems to fit this situation perfectly."

"Still, Nessie, it's—"

"A moot point, so let's get moving. First, we need to stop at Stooge's."

Seamus is not as nice to me as Ness was. He's beyond livid and believes I should have told her everything the second she woke up. I can't remember the number of times Seamus called me egit' wanker during our conversation. If you're unfamiliar with Irish slang, he said I'm an idiot who wasted an opportunity. I don't disagree with him.

He's also worried she may have found another job or worse since she's missed her last two shifts and didn't answer the door when he stopped by earlier today.

Knowing where we need to go next. I knock on the front door once, but when Shay doesn't answer, I don't waste any more time waiting. Grabbing the knob, I twist hard until I hear it break, granting us access to the place she has called home since right after she moved here. I will replace the lock later.

We move through room after room, finding it mostly undisturbed but lacking any of her personal items. It's like she was never here. And this thought leaves an empty feeling inside me.

She left you, you fucking asshole. We lost her, all because you refused to tell her how much she meant to us. I will never forgive you for this. Shadow groans before falling completely silent.

When I come back into the main living space, Ness is standing by the table, her focus dropped to the paper in her hand. When she lifts her head, I discover eyes brimming with tears as she holds it out for me.

Seamus, if you're reading this, you already know the truth that I left without saying goodbye. Cowardly, right? I'm aware, and I'm sorry. I put next month's rent in the little drawer in the kitchen. I figured it was the least I could do. After everything you have done for me, I know I owe you some answers. I just don't think I have it in me to always wonder what could have been. Living without him (this last word is scribbled out and replaced with two others), my pack was harder than I thought, so I have decided to go home. Thank you for everything you have done. I'm sorry I didn't have the guts to do this in person. Goddess knows you deserve it. Tell Hyde I'll miss his smiling face. I truly wish I had the fortitude to see you both one more time. To thank you for your kindness. To make sure you both understand, when I lost all faith in everyone, you restored it, but I'm not sure I could leave if I did this in person. Tell Ness and Finch they did everything to help make me feel at home, but ultimately, this isn't my home. And tell Foster I wish him the best and hope he finds the happiness he deserves someday soon. And please tell everyone else I said bye. With all my love, Shay.

"She's gone."

"I see that."

"And you're okay with it?"

"I don't have a choice. She never asked me what I wanted, and it seems Shay has made her decision."

"Bullshit. You're being an ass. Seamus is right; you should have told Shay the truth right away. You never should have let her believe she didn't mean anything to you."

"She had to have known."

"Known what? Every time she was within earshot of you, the only thing she heard was you saying how you had no intention of being with her. Or how you didn't want to be around her. What the hell was she supposed to think, Foster?"

Looking down at the note in my hand, I focus on the part she wrote for me. She hopes I find my happiness. Finding any contentment in my life has never seemed farther away than it

179

does now. Hell, Shadow's silence alone is deafening. Seeing her words to me finally snaps everything into place as I lay the paper on the table and turn to go.

"What are you doing?"

"What I should have done a long time ago."

"Which is?"

"Beg my mate not to give up on me."

Note from Author: If you have enjoyed Season Two, please consider leaving a review. Season Three is already well underway on Kindle Vella, with new episodes released every Monday and Thursday. You can follow me on Facebook, TikTok, Instagram, and Goodreads for any upcoming projects. In the meantime, if you are looking for another all-consuming Paranormal Romance, check out my other books. The Scarred by Fate Series is available through Amazon, Kindle, or my newest release, Death's Inquest, book one in the Arrival of the Four Horsemen series. Until we meet again for season three, Happy Reading.

Also by *Marcelle Valentine*

Scarred by Fate Series
Ritual Nightmare
Breaking Purgatory
Fate's Ritual
Opposing Tartarus
Sacrificial Endings

The Ash Rock Series
Shadow's Moon Season One
Shadow's Moon Season Two
Shadow's Moon Season Three
Shadow's Moon Season Four

Arrival of the Four Horsemen Series
Death's Inquest
Pestilence's Judgment
War's Verdict
Coming Soon Famine's Punishment

Kindle Vella
Shadow's Moon Season One through Four
Seized by Sin
Silverwood Throne

Teaser

What do you do when a demon is chasing you?

Fall in love with a supernatural who is hellbent on saving you.

Gift or Everything?

Amidst the chaos of my life, I question whether I am a demon's gift or Logan's everything.

I have spent most of my life running from the demon my father summoned, and now I find myself in a small town. This simple life is a welcomed change from the endless hum of dread that has been my constant companion. I pray I can stay longer than a few months this time, however my past tells me these prayers will go unanswered.

Until I stumble across Logan, and everything changes. His presence is consuming, and I can't help but be drawn to him. His shifting eyes are both thrilling and mesmerizing. The feeling of safety that washes over me when I'm with him is unlike anything I have ever experienced. It's as if I'm finally home after years of wandering.

The longer I'm around him, the more I realize Logan is not just a man. Whenever he's near, there is an inexplicable power emanating from him that is both exhilarating and terrifying. Logic tells me to run, while my heart tells me to stay.

Marcelle Valentine

Acknowledgments

When I began this project, I figured it would be a short story, something I could use as a starting point on Kindle Vella. I never knew how much I would learn to love the characters or how much they would have to say. Currently, season three is underway on Kindle Vella, and what I imagine is the fourth and final season releasing this Spring 2023. Each season will come to Kindle and Kindle Unlimited 30 days after the season completes on Vella. If you decide you cannot wait to continue their story, jump over to Kindle Vella to catch up with the gang from Ash Rock.

My deepest heartfelt thanks go out to every reader who took a chance on an unknown author and gave this series a chance. I hope you got lost in their world, if only for a minute in time.

I could not have completed this without the people who supported me, including my beta readers, my niece Ashley, my mom, and my daughter Melanie. Everything you each did to help me bring this project to life is something I could never say thank you enough. You each poured your time into this to help me make it something worth reading.

I have several projects underway, with the first one in my horsemen series, Death's Inquest, releasing on January 27th.

Thank you to my husband and everyone else in my family who have been my biggest cheerleaders. I love every one of you.

And finally, to every author that has ever put pen to paper, fingers to keyboard, whose work only inspired me more to follow this dream, I hope I do not disappoint.

Thank you
Marcelle

Marcelle Valentine

Newsletter

Consider visiting my website and signing up for my newsletter to receive updates on this series and all my future projects.

www. marcellevalentine.com

Please consider leaving a review on Amazon and Goodreads if you enjoyed the book. Any thoughts are appreciated and will only help me improve the story. Reviews also provide new readers with a way to find my books.

You can also follow me on social media

Facebook
Goodreads
Instagram
TikTok

Marcelle Valentine

About the Author

Marcelle Valentine has long been an admirer of creating worlds in which people can get lost. From a young age, her active imagination took her on epic journeys to faraway places where troubles and friendships abound. After discovering the intriguing world of Paranormal/Fantasy Romance, which stirred up memories of all those distant places and friends, her desire to write returned. She invites you to travel with her during these journeys and get lost in a world with friends, enemies, and lovers, all firmly rooted in the supernatural realm. Marcelle is the author of the Scarred by Fate Series and the episodic series Shadow's Moon. She lives in Ohio with her husband. She has two children, three grandchildren, and one lovable, lazy Great Dane.

Marcellevalentine. com

Facebook

Goodreads

Instagram

TikTok

www.ingramcontent.com/pod-product-compliance
Lightning Source LLC
Chambersburg PA
CBHW061232170626
46809CB00007B/2635